Claudia Kishi, Live From WSTO!

**Other books by
Ann M. Martin**

Claudia Kishi, Live From WSTO!

Ann M. Martin

AN
APPLE
PAPERBACK

SCHOLASTIC INC.
New York Toronto London Auckland Sydney

Cover art by Hodges Soileau

ISBN 0-590-48236-X

12 11 10 9 8 7 6 5 4 3 2 1   5 6 7 8 9/9 0/0

Printed in the U.S.A.   40

First Scholastic printing, May 1995

The author gratefully acknowledges
Peter Lerangis
for his help in
preparing this manuscript.

Claudia Kishi, Live From WSTO!

CHAPTER 1

"So the bases are loaded, okay? The score is tied, two outs — and the batter hits a slow grounder to Jake Kuhn at first. . . ."

Kristy Thomas was talking.

And talking.

Me? I was working hard. Trying to keep my eyes open. If I fell asleep, my face would land in my lunch. And I did not want to go to my next class with hair full of chipped beef with cream sauce.

Baseball is not my favorite topic. It's not rock bottom, but it's pretty close. If Kristy had been talking about spelling, or techniques of room cleaning, my nose would already have been in the beef.

"So what do you think Jake does?" Kristy looked around. Her face was all a-twinkle, as if we were on the edges of our seats.

Now, if you were talking, and you saw three droopy-eyed girls staring back at you, slowly

1

chewing their meals, would you assume they were dying of suspense?

"Give up? *He fields the ball and runs home!*"

Chew, chew, chew. We raised our eyebrows and tried to seem fascinated.

"Maybe he had to go to the bathroom," I suggested. "Those games are long."

Kristy looked at me blankly for a moment, then snapped, "Home *plate*, Claudia! See, he wanted to stop the run, even though all he had to do was step on first. Which would have ended the game without a run scored!"

Oh.

The chipped beef was looming closer.

Kristy, as you can guess, is a sports fanatic. She's the founder, manager, and head coach of Kristy's Krushers, a softball team for little kids.

Are you sitting down? I, Claudia Kishi, Dunce of All Sports, was once the co-coach of the Krushers. Yes, it's true. When Kristy joined the Stoneybrook Middle School softball team and didn't have time to coach, my friend Stacey McGill and I took her place.

It didn't help. I still don't know how to play the game.

"Well," Kristy said grumpily, "I guess you had to be there."

She took her fork and began shoveling in her lunch, as if she hadn't eaten in days.

"Ew, Kristy, please eat with your mouth closed," Dawn said. "Who wants to watch you chew up murdered mammals?"

Kristy burst out laughing so hard, I thought she was going to hurl. *Murdered mammals?*

"Well, that meat in your mouth was once a living, feeling cow." Dawn lifted a forkful of lettuce and pointed it at Kristy for emphasis. "Have you ever seen photos of what happens inside a slaughterhouse? The poor, shivering beasts heading toward their death — "

"Dawn, please," Mary Anne said.

I pushed my lunch aside. Suddenly I wasn't hungry.

Kristy shrugged. "Some people collect dolls. Some collect baseball cards. Dawn Schafer collects pictures of cow torture."

"Can we change the subject?" I asked.

"Yes!" Mary Anne agreed. "Um . . . Logan and I are making a tape tonight. You know, a collection of our favorite songs."

"I did that once," Kristy said.

"Thirty-two renditions of 'Take Me Out to the Ball Game,' " I remarked. (Sorry, it just slipped out of my mouth.)

Kristy pelted me with a roll.

Don't worry. Kristy and I are friends. If she didn't like me, she would have thrown something harder.

3

Actually, Kristy has pelted me with a lot of things over the years. We grew up across the street from each other here in Stoneybrook, Connecticut. My mom says Kristy used to bop me with her Raggedy Ann because I didn't learn to walk as fast as she did. (Figures.)

As I walked home from school that afternoon in the spring sunshine, my jacket slung over my shoulder, I wished Kristy still lived in her old house. On gorgeous afternoons like these, she had all kinds of great outdoorsy plans.

"Hi, Janine!" I called to my sister as I breezed in the front door and through the living room.

"Hello, — " I was halfway up the stairs when Janine saw me. "Claudia, what on Earth are you wearing?"

Gulp.

I was wearing a backward T-shirt, overalls I'd made by sewing together two halves cut from different pairs, and mismatched socks. It was my "deconstructionist" look. You know, like the art movement? Those paintings that show you the parts of objects rearranged in interesting ways? Well, that was the idea, anyway. Cool, huh?

I am obsessed with art. Painting, sculpture, drawing, jewelry-making — I like to create in any medium. Including clothes. (This makes me Chief Oddball in my family. For my parents, tasseled loafers are daring.)

Janine shook her head, chuckling. "Was *that* why you wore your jacket to breakfast this morning? To cover that up so we wouldn't have indigestion?"

"I was *cold*." (Well, it was sort of true.)

Janine just shook her head and walked to her room.

Later I could hear the usual furious clacking of the computer keyboard coming from Janine's room. I tried to slip quietly by her open door, to avoid another comment.

"Hm. Frankenstein's jumpsuit," I heard as I entered my bedroom.

Janine is disgustingly smart. Even if she lent me, like, one quarter of her IQ points, I'd be brilliant and she'd still have enough left over to be a genius. She is a high school sophomore, but she takes college courses. And her taste in fashion runs to white blouses and gray pleated skirts.

Needless to say, my parents think she's perfect.

I've tried to be a high achiever like her. But 1) I can't spell, 2) computers hate me (and vice versa), and 3) my eyes cross when I read anything more complicated than a Nancy Drew mystery.

Where did my artistic side come from? Probably my mom's mom, Mimi. She understood me better than anyone else. Mimi's English wasn't great (she immigrated to this country from Japan), but it didn't matter. We were on the same wavelength. She lived with us my whole life and I loved her *soooo* much. When she died I was devastated.

Actually, one other person inherited the crazy, creative genes in my family—my aunt Peaches, Mimi's other daughter. (Her real name is Miyoshi. Her husband, my uncle Russ, gave her the nickname. Why? No one knows.) When Peaches was pregnant, she and Russ bought a house in Stoneybrook. While they waited for the occupants to move out, they lived with us for a month. It was a wild and mostly fun time, but it ended sadly. You see, Peaches had a miscarriage.

Russ and Peaches moved into their new house anyway, and they're still planning to have another baby. Now Peaches works full-time. I really miss her.

Now our house is pretty quiet. Dull, if you want to know the truth. Except during Baby-sitters Club meetings, which are held in my room.

But you know what? With Stacey McGill gone, even those are less fun.

No, Stacey didn't move away. She quit (or was fired, depending on who's telling the story, but more about that later).

Mimi, Peaches, Stacey. My three soulmates. Without them in my life, I was feeling a little bummed.

Not that I don't love my other BSC friends. I do. I'm lucky to have them. But you know how it is. You need that one extra-special person in your life.

Sigh.

Time for a pick-me-up. A definite Twinkie moment. I opened my desk drawer and peeked under a stack of looseleaf papers.

Only one box of Milk Duds and two Snickers bars.

I rummaged under my bed, where I discovered three bags of pretzels and some Charleston Chews. I opened a few shoe boxes in my closet, which contained M&M's and Raisinets and Yankee Doodles and Doritos.

I finally found a Twinkie among my art supplies. I ripped open the wrapper and ate.

I felt much better.

Why do I hide my junk food? Because of my parents, also known as the Nutrition Police. They disapprove of unhealthy food, which is probably why I love it so much. Besides, I'm in pretty good shape, and I eat my dinner every night without complaining, so what's the diff?

As I chewed, I changed clothes. That afternoon I had a short sitting job at the Pikes'. They have eight kids (one of whom is a BSC member, thank goodness), so there's already enough deconstruction in that house.

Besides, I didn't want to catch a snide remark on the way out.

Dressed in jeans and a button-down men's shirt over a stretch top, I walked to the Pikes'. I brought a Kid-Kit with me. (Well, sort of.) Kid-Kits are supposed to be boxes full of toys, games, and activities for kids. (Kristy thought of the idea, and kids really do love them.) Mine, though, is filled with art supplies. It's more of an Art-Kit.

Slate Street was silent. This is unusual, because the Pikes live there. The neighbors must have been in shock.

Claire Pike, who's five, answered the door.

"Hi! Hi! Hi! Hi! Hi! Hi! Hi!" she squealed, jumping up and down.

"Come on in, Claudia!" Mallory Pike shouted from the den. Mal's the oldest Pike (eleven). She's the BSC member I mentioned. "We're having story time."

Claire raced into the den ahead of me. She sat on the floor next to her triplet brothers, Adam, Jordan, and Byron Pike.

Yes, ten-year-old boy triplets. Yikes! Can you imagine? And that, of course, is just the beginning of the Pikes. The others are Vanessa (nine), Nicky (eight), Margo (seven), and Claire the Jumping Bean.

And they were all, *all*, staring quietly at Mallory and a hairy monster.

The hairy monster looked suspiciously like Ben Hobart, with a mask. (Ben is Mal's boyfriend, more or less.)

"And so the horrible Oogly Oogly Beast searched high and low for his missing toothbrush," Mal read from a spiral notebook. "He had not brushed his teeth for days. . . ."

"Ewww," Byron Pike said. "Bad breath!"

Behind Mal, Ben the Beast put his hands on his hips and tried to look angry.

Mal went on, and I listened. With her reddish-brown hair pulled back into a thick ponytail, and her big, round glasses, she looked older than eleven. Her story was about a monster who was obsessed with being clean. (Mal is a great writer, and she wants to be a children's author/illustrator someday.)

I sat on the floor and started doodling. I tried to make some illustrations for Mallory's story, but they looked kind of stupid. So I watched.

" . . . So the Oogly Oogly Beast slooooowly approached the campers. Drool dripped from his mouth and onto his white fur. Then, bursting into the campsite, he shouted — "

Mallory paused. Ben froze in an attack position.

"What? What?" Vanessa demanded.

Mallory's eyes widened threateningly. Then she said, " 'Uh, excuse me, does anybody have a Wash'n Dri?' "

The kids cracked up.

Mallory grinned at Ben. I could hear him laughing behind his mask.

The two of them were very cute. And all of a sudden I had another reminder of why I was feeling rotten.

Boylessness.

Mary Anne had Logan. Mallory had Ben. Kristy (sort of) had this boy named Bart. Stacey, my ex-best friend, had a boyfriend named Robert.

Claudia? Zilch.

Not that I'm boy-crazed. It's no great tragedy not to have a boyfriend.

But, hey, it's no great honor either.

I've tried. I even placed an ad in the personals column in the Stoneybrook Middle School newspaper. I was *running* the column at the time, but that didn't help. The only people who answered my appeal for the "Perfect Boy" were Alan Gray (the class geek) and Stacey McGill. (Yes, Stacey. She was feeling sorry for me.)

Sometimes I wish I were still working on

the newspaper. At least I'd be meeting people.

"Waaaaahhhhh!" Ben was crying now.

"Poor, poor Oogly," Mallory said. "All those teeth and nothing to brush with . . ."

Poor, poor Claudia, I thought.

"No bathtub, no towel . . ."

No boyfriend, no best friend, no activities . . .

"So sad and lonely . . ."

So sad and lonely.

Puh-leeze. Get a grip, Kishi.

I stood up and left the room. I tried to look nonchalant about it.

But boy, was I feeling sorry for myself.

By the time I reached the kitchen, I had made up my mind. I needed a change. I was going to do something new with my life. Something interesting. Fun. Different.

By the end of the day, I, Claudia Kishi, was going to turn my life around!

CHAPTER 2

I lied.

My life was exactly the same, right through to the next day, Wednesday.

But I'd been trying. After I left the Pikes, I mentioned my problem at home. Janine suggested taking computer programming. Dad brought up stamp collecting. Mom's response was, "Don't you have homework?"

Big help.

So I sat down and made a list of possible choices — the first things that came to mind, no matter how strange.

1. Tuba
2. tap dancing
3. Cooking
4. ~~cor~~ Chorrus
5. Swiming
6. dramma club

The next morning, I began testing the waters.

I tried making an omelet in the microwave. It tasted like plastic with cheese sauce.

Scratch number 3.

At school I took a look at a tuba. It was love at first sight. *Sooo* cool. Then I imagined taking it home to practice.

Ugh. Number 1 was out. (I'd have to take weightlifting first.)

I asked the music teacher about chorus, and she told me I needed to come in after school and sing for her. Alone.

I said thanks but no thanks. Flush number 4.

I was going to talk to the captain of the SMS swim team, until I took a look at her chlorine-damaged hair. NFM! (*Not For Me.*)

Number 5 bit the dust.

That left tap and drama. I was once involved in a production of *Peter Pan*, but only as a set designer. And I knew nothing about tap. Fortunately one of my BSC friends, Jessica Ramsey, is an excellent dancer. Several BSC members have sung and acted in shows. (Kristy played the lead in *Peter Pan*, and Shannon Kilbourne has starred in summer camp musicals.)

I figured I'd bring up choices 2 and 6 at the Baby-sitters Club meeting.

So after school, I went home and waited.

That's the nice thing about living in the exclusive headquarters of your club. Everyone comes to you. (Plus you are almost never late.)

What makes the Claudia Kishi bedroom so special? My scintillating personality? My superior art? My confectionary collection?

Well, yes, of course. But mostly my phone. I'm the only BSC member with a private line, which is crucial to our business.

Yes, business. We all have titles and duties. (I'm the vice-president and official off-hours phone answerer.) Our clients are Stoneybrook parents, who call us during out meeting times — five-thirty to six, every Monday, Wednesday, and Friday. With one phone call, they reach six great baby-sitters. That's the way the BSC works.

I mean, *duh*, what a simple idea, right? Wrong. No one had thought of it before Kristy Thomas.

Kristy is an Idea Machine. I mean it. She is not normal. If she put her mind to it, she could figure out how to de-stripe a tiger. She dreamed up the BSC one afternoon when her mom couldn't find a sitter for her little brother, David Michael.

Times were tough for Kristy's family back then. Mrs. Thomas was raising four kids by herself — Charlie (who's now seventeen), Sam

14

(fifteen), and David Michael (seven and a half). Kristy's dad had walked out on his family not long after David Michael was born, just left them flat, no explanations, no nothing. Can you imagine?

Boy, have things changed. Mrs. Thomas married this nice, quiet guy named Watson Brewer, who is a millionaire. Now Kristy and her family live in a real mansion on the wealthy side of town, along with an adopted little sister, Emily Michelle, who's from Vietnam; Nannie, Kristy's grandmother; Watson's two kids from his previous marriage (seven-year-old Karen and four-year-old Andrew, who are there every other month); and several pets.

Now that Kristy lives so far away, she has to be driven to meetings by her brother, Charlie. Even so, she has hardly ever been late to a meeting. In fact, she's usually the first one there.

That day, she arrived at 5:24.

"Hey, Claudia, what's up?" she said.

"Ohhh, *up*town, *up*state . . ." I answered cheerfully. (Not bad, huh? I had just thought of it.)

"Groan." Kristy rolled her eyes and sat in the director's chair near my desk. That's her usual spot. (Mine is on my bed, sitting cross-legged.)

"Kristy," I said, "I need an activity, something really interesting and fun. And don't tell me to take a sport — "

"DON'T WORRY, I WON'T UPSET YOU." Kristy spoke in this exaggerated, loud voice, then started laughing and slapping her knees.

"Uh, Kristy? Are you okay?"

"*Up*set! Get it? *Up* . . . set!"

I love Kristy. Really. But there's another side to that incredible brain.

She's competitive. Even with jokes. Sometimes she just doesn't know when to stop.

I smiled patiently. "Uh-huh. Um, listen, Kristy. What do you think I should take, tap or drama?"

Kristy looked at me as if I'd suggested adding another nose to my face. "Are you serious? What about something like volleyball?"

Fortunately Jessi Ramsey and Mallory Pike walked in the room then. Jessi's eleven, like Mal. They are our two sixth-grade members (the rest of us are eighth-graders).

I explained my situation. Well, almost all of it. I didn't say I felt sad and friendless, just that I needed a change of pace.

Jessi was all smiles when I mentioned tap. "Stand up. I'll give you a lesson," she said.

"Now?" I asked.

"Before the others get here. Come on, hold onto the side of your desk."

I did.

"Okay, watch." She began shifting from side to side. "Ball *change*, ball *change*. . . ."

I tried to copy her. It wasn't hard to do, but I looked like a total geek.

When she started doing things called shuffles and falaps, I was hopeless.

The problem is, Jessi is practically a pro. She takes all kinds of dance lessons. (Ballet is her specialty. She's performed lead roles in productions at her ballet school.) She even looks like a dancer. She's thin and graceful, with turned-out feet.

Jessi and Mal are our junior officers. Neither of them is allowed to baby-sit during the evenings, unless it's for their own siblings (and boy, do they complain about *that*), but they do a lot of sitting on afternoons and weekends. They are absolute best friends. They are also certified horse fanatics (I think they have memorized the plot of every single *Saddle Club* book).

Like Mal, Jessi's the oldest in her family, and is convinced that her parents treat her like a baby. Unlike Mal, Jessi has a normal-sized family, with two siblings. Also, Jessi's African-American and Mal's white.

"No, no!" Jessi was saying to me. "You shift your weight on a falap. That's what makes it different from a shuffle!"

Uh-huh.

My dreams of stardom were flying out the window.

By now, the rest of the members of the BSC had arrived. I figured we could settle down and forget I even mentioned tap.

But noooo. Shannon Kilbourne and Dawn Schafer were holding onto a bookshelf and doing perfect falaps (or maybe shuffles). Kristy was trying to imitate them, but her tap-dancing looked like soccer practice.

Only Mary Anne Spier had the good sense to stay seated.

"Come on, Mary Anne," Kristy urged her.

"I, uh, have to do some updating," Mary Anne replied, blushing. She was holding the BSC record book in front of her, like a shield.

Mary Anne blushes a lot. She's the shyest, sweetest, most sensitive person on earth. Also the most organized. Which makes her a perfect club secretary. You should see that record book. In her neat handwriting, she fills a calendar with all our jobs and conflicts (doctor and dentist appointments, family trips, Kristy's practices, Jessi's dance classes, and so on). She also keeps an up-to-date client list, with addresses, phone numbers, rates charged, and special needs, likes, and dislikes of the kids we sit for. And, believe it or not, she *enjoys* doing this!

Like Kristy, Mary Anne used to live on my street. You'd never think those two opposites would be best friends, but they are. Actually, they do have things in common. Both are short and brown-haired. And they both had pretty sad lives that changed for the better.

Mary Anne's mom died when Mary Anne was a baby. Her dad raised her by himself, and he went overboard with rules. Right through seventh grade Mary Anne had a super-early curfew, and she had to wear little-girl clothes and keep her hair in pigtails.

Mr. Spier began to loosen up a little over time. But things really changed when Dawn Schafer moved to town. See, Dawn's mom used to be sweethearts with Mary Anne's dad, back when they went to Stoneybrook High School. But Dawn's grandparents thought he was too low-class or something, so the romance went kersplat. Dawn's mom moved to California, married a guy named Jack Schafer, had Dawn and her younger brother, divorced her husband, and came back to Stoneybrook. By that time, Mrs. Schafer had forgotten about her old boyfriend Richard Spier. Then Dawn became close to Mary Anne, and together they found out about their parents' long-ago romance. So . . . Dawn and Mary Anne matched them up again. And we all cried at the wedding.

Mary Anne and her dad moved into the Schafers' farmhouse, which is two hundred years old and extremely cool. Now the Schafer/Spiers are one big, happy family.

Sort of.

Dawn's brother, Jeff, hated Stoneybrook. From the moment he moved here, he was miserable and homesick. Mrs. Schafer finally let him move back to California to live with his dad, and he's been much happier.

Recently Dawn became homesick, too. So *she* went back to California, but only for a few months. (During that time her dad remarried, and Kristy, Mary Anne, and I went to the wedding.)

Dawn and I are *sooooo* different. Physically, for one thing. Her hair is practically white, and she has light, freckled skin. Another big difference is our taste in food. Now, I have nothing against healthy eating. Seriously. I do eat unjunky food. But I just don't understand how anyone could get excited about tofu. (Have you ever tasted the stuff? It's like eating warm socks.)

Dawn can get excited about it, though. Plus she gets excited about non-food things such as global warming, ozone layers, rain forests, and animal testing. She is such an independent thinker. She doesn't care what anyone else thinks of her.

20

As alternate officer, Dawn takes over whenever another member is absent. Lately she's been our treasurer, since Stacey left the BSC.

Which brings me to the story of Stacey.

Okay. First of all, Stacey is (or *was*) a very cool girl, and one of the original BSC members. She has gorgeous golden-blonde hair, and an incredible sense of style — sophisticated and urban and up-to-the-second. She was born and raised in New York City, and she often visits her dad there (the McGills are divorced).

Anyway, Stacey recently met this guy, Robert Brewster, who's cute, athletic, smart, and sensitive. Plus he's in LUV with her. So, naturally, Stacey began spending a lot of time with him and his friends. But then she started arriving late to BSC meetings. And backing out of jobs. And acting superior to other BSC members. And not inviting club members to a party at her house (*I* was the only one invited, which made me feel weird).

Then came the Big Fight. Everyone blew up at Stace during a BSC meeting (and vice versa). She quit and Kristy fired her at the same time.

I was pretty mad at Stacey then. I still don't hang out with her, but I've calmed down. I've started saying hi to her in school. (The other club members don't, which I think is kind of immature.)

I wish Stacey had never met Robert. I have

nothing against him. Or against her. It's just the situation. I miss Stacey, especially at our meetings. I could picture her that Wednesday, trying to tap dance. She'd probably be just as klutzy as the rest of us, but she'd look great.

"Uh, guys," I said to the thundering herd. "I don't think I'm cut out for this."

"No, you're fine!" Jessi insisted.

But before Jessi could show me another way to look like a klutz, my clock radio clicked to five-thirty.

"Okay, enough," Kristy harrumphed. "This meeting of the Baby-sitters Club will come to order!"

Panting for breath, we all sat down.

"The first order of business," Kristy said, "is Claudia's problem. Okay. You've had a tap lesson. Now, Shannon and I would be happy to give you a drama lesson."

Drama lesson?

"Whoa," I protested. "Can't we just, like, talk about it?"

"You bet," Kristy replied. "Shannon, you have the floor first."

Thank you, Kristy Thomas, talk-show host.

Shannon, by the way, is one of our two associate members (the other is Logan). Associates aren't required to attend meetings, but Shannon's been helping out since Stacey left. Shannon goes to a private school called Stoneybrook Day. (The rest of us go to Stoneybrook Middle School.) She's in tons of extracurricular activities there, including drama club.

"Well, we started *You Can't Take It With You*," Shannon said. "Right now we're just blocking, though."

"Not the football kind," Kristy remarked. Duh.

"No. Blocking is mapping out all the movements. Entrances, exits. Stuff like that has to be precise. It's like choreography, sort of."

"I remember seeing some of that in *Peter Pan* rehearsals. Is it hard?" I asked.

"A little. All your moves happen on specific lines of the dialogue. You mark down all the moves in your script. You memorize your cue lines. Then, after you've memorized your own lines, you've memorized the blocking, too."

Right. Sure. Gee, that sounded easy.

I might as well join the math club.

"What happens if you forget your lines during a performance?" I asked.

Shannon smiled. "That's called 'going up.' The actor's nightmare. Happens to everybody."

Oh, yeah? Well, not to me.

My list was a bust. Zero for six.

The rest of the meeting was pretty busy with phone calls. We didn't talk much more about my problem. Which was okay. I didn't want to make it seem like a big deal.

Ease up, Kishi, I told myself. Life wasn't so bad.

Just dull.

I said good-bye to everyone, then flopped onto my bed. In about ten minutes, I'd have to start helping with dinner. Not enough time for homework, and I didn't feel in an artistic mood.

I flicked on my clock radio. It was tuned, as always, to the local radio station, WSTO. A rock song was playing, and I listened to the end of it. My eyes started feeling heavy. I could feel myself dozing off.

"And that was U 4 Me, rockin' it for you here on WSTO!" chirped this goony-sounding deejay. "We'll have more music for you in a minute, but first let me tell you about our *coooooool connnntesssssssst. . . .*"

Those last two words were full of echo or reverb or whatever they call that. It was giving me a headache. I reached out to turn the radio off.

"Say, kids, if you've been listening to me and thinking, 'Hey, I could do that,' well, here's your chance. *You* can be the host of your own show on WSTO. A kids' show. That's right. If you're between the ages of ten and fourteen — that's years, ha ha — you can have your own one-hour radio show, twice a week for . . . a fuuullll monnnnnth!"

My hand froze.

"You find the guests," he went on. "You plan and emcee the show. It's all up to you, if you're the winner of our Host of the Month Contest! To enter, just tell us why we should hire you — on one sheet of paper, please. Make it serious, make it funny, make it *you*! Don't forget to include your name, age, address, and a description of yourself and your interests. We'll announce the winner on Monday, so hurry. And now, more *greaaaat muuuusic*!"

My mind was in warp speed.

My very own radio show? Me, Claudia Kishi, a deejay?

Yes. I could see it.

This was it.

This was what I was looking for!

CHAPTER 3

I wuld like to be a kids radio show hoast becaus I have alot of expiriense with kids and

Look no more. I, Claudia Kishi am exacly the person you want. Youl'l be sorry if you

Hi. Im Claudia Kishi, but my freinds call me Claud. WSTO is a cool stacion. And I mean that.

The position of Hoste is of grat importanse expeshelly considering the rabbid listeners who so intensly listen

No. No. No.

Everything sounded awful.

I dropped my pen, propped up my elbows on my desk, and buried my face in my hands.

Think, Claudia!

What had happened to me? I used to be a pretty decent writer. Seriously. When I was doing my Personals column for the *SMS Express*, I had to deal with tons of horribly written personal ads. Sometimes I'd rewrite them from scratch. First I'd figure out exactly what the person was trying to say. Then I'd cut out the words that weren't necessary.

The essentials. That's what I needed

The brilliance would come later.

I wrote out a list. Just short sentence fragments. Exactly why I wanted the job.

Then I worked on putting it all together into an essay. I tried to keep it short, sweet, and really *me*.

I consumed a Milky Way, a box of Peppermint Patties, two Chunkies, and half a bag of Cape Cod potato chips.

Finally I had to go to sleep. My brain was fried. (My stomach didn't feel too great either.)

I worked on the essay the next morning, before I went to school. Then, during lunch, I convinced Emily Bernstein (the *SMS Express*'s student editor) to let me use the newspaper's word processor for my final draft.

I typed my essay out carefully. Then I closed my eyes, held my breath, and prepared for the worst part.

Spellcheck.

My spelling stinks. The computer went wild. It must have stopped at a hundred misspelled words. I thought it would crash from overwork.

But when it was done, my essay looked like this:

WHY I WANT TO BE
~~R~~O HOST OF THE MONTH

by Claudia Kishi

Here is my idea of a great host for a kids' show:

Someone who's not shy but is also a good listener. Someone who knows what kind of music, fashion, and jokes kids like. Someone who understands the problems and concerns of kids of all ages. And most of all, someone who's reliable and hard-working.

And that someone is me, Claudia Kishi!

Okay, first of all, let me say right out, I don't have any radio experience. But I'm an expert at talking. Just ask any of my friends. (On second thought, don't. Take my word for it!)

As for reliable and hard-working? Well, I baby-sit a lot. In fact, I'm vice-president of a baby-sitters club that meets three times a week. I also used to run a column in the Stoneybrook Middle School newspaper, called Claudia's Personals.

From my column and my baby-sitting, I've learned a lot. I think I know what kids like — from infants right on up to eighth graders!

I once heard an old saying that went, "Having an open mind is one thing, but letting bats fly around inside it is something else entirely." Well, my mind is open to the experience of a radio show. But the only things flying around inside it are my ideas for programming. I can't wait to share them with you!

Not bad, huh? Serious but humorous, not too stiff, well-spelled. And it's always nice to throw in a little quotation. (I'd been dying to use that one. I read it in a book once, and I think it is so cool.)

"Good afternoon, this is Claudia Kishi on WSTO," I said as I pressed the print key.

Whoa, did that feel good! I started giggling.

Then I forced myself to stop. *Do not NOT NOT get your hopes up*, I thought. Probably dozens — hundreds — of kids would be entering. Kids who deejayed in summer camp. Whose parents were in the radio business. Who worked on school "radio stations" broadcast over P.A. systems. Who could write Pulitzer Prize-winning essays.

I had to be realistic.

One thing was sure: I did not want anyone to know about this. That way, if I won, I could surprise them all with the good news, but if I lost, I could just keep the humiliation to myself.

I took the essay out of the printer, folded it, and put it in an envelope. Before I stuck it in my shoulder bag, I gave it a little kiss.

"Tomorrow we expect a high in the low fifties, cooler by the Sound . . ."

It was Monday, 5:29. I was in my bedroom, along with the other members of the BSC, listening to my clock radio. Well, *I* was listening to the radio. Everyone else was gabbing about I don't know what.

I was a train wreck. For five days I had not stopped thinking about my essay. I rewrote it over and over in my mind. I couldn't sleep.

And now, the Big Day had arrived. Today the winner was going to be announced.

When? On which show? I had no idea. I hadn't paid attention to that part.

Which meant I had to listen to everything.

Beeeeep. "WSTO news time is five-thirty," said the announcer.

"Order!" barked Kristy.

I managed to zap myself back into reality.

Dawn held up the BSC's "treasury," a manila envelope. "Dues day!"

Everyone muttered and grunted and reached for money. (No complaining from me, though. I don't mind dues. Mainly because they help pay my phone bill.)

"And now, from the sixties," the WSTO deejay was saying, "an old, moldy, good, and goldy! Here are the Beatles with — "

"Claudia, could you turn that thing off?" Kristy said.

"I love the Beatles!" I blurted out. (Okay, I was exaggerating.)

"Since when?" Kristy asked.

"Well, uh, okay, I'll lower it." I turned the knob (slightly) and changed the subject. "Um, anybody want Skittles?"

"Me! Me!" a chorus of voices answered.

"Yeah, yeah, yeah," the Beatles wailed.

I dug the Skittles out of my sock drawer. No one seemed to mind the song much. Soon it was business as usual — munch, gab, gab, munch. I kept quiet, my ears tuned to the radio.

The phone must have rung, because I noticed Kristy snatching up the receiver. "Hello, Baby-sitters Club," she said. "Okay. We'll call you right back." Then she hung up and announced, "We need two sitters for the Barrett/DeWitt kids on Saturday."

Mary Anne looked in the record book. "Let's see, Dawn's free, and so are you, Kristy."

Kristy called Mrs. DeWitt back. "It'll be me and Dawn, Mrs. DeWitt. . . . Okay, 'bye."

Kristy hung up. The radio droned on: "We have a three-mile backup on Route Ninety-Five. . . ."

Kristy yawned. Jessi and Mal were playing Hangman on the floor. Mary Anne was scribbling in the notebook. Dawn and Shannon were looking at a magazine.

And I was listening to: " . . . allow at least a half hour leaving Stamford to the east . . ."

Kristy reached for the radio. "This is giving me a headache."

"No, don't!" I snapped.

Rrrrrrinnnng!

Saved by the phone. I leaned over the radio, blocking Kristy, and picked up the receiver. "Hello, Baby-sitters Club!" I said.

"Yes, hello, dear. This is Ginger Wilder, and I was wondering if someone was free on — "

"And now we have for you the winner of our *Host of the Month contest . . . ontest . . . ontest . . .*" the announcer intoned (with *lots* of reverb).

"Aaaagh! Mrs. Wilder, can I call you back?" I said.

"Oh, my. Is something wrong?" Mrs. Wilder asked.

"About five minutes, okay? Sorry!"

"Fine. I'll be h — "

Click.

I hung up. I cannot believe how rude I was. Around me were six dropped jaws and twelve bewildered eyes.

I turned up the radio. "We have read them all," the announcer said. "And they were ter-rrrrr*ific*! But we believe we have a winner. The first place essay for the WSTO *Ho-o-o-o-st* of the Month contest was written by . . ."

A drumroll began. I wanted to die. I was sitting there with my stomach inside out, and they were playing a *drumroll*!

"Would you mind telling us what is going on here?" Kristy said testily.

"Sssshhhh!" I hissed.

"*Claaaaaaaaudia Kishiiiiiiiiii!*" blared the announcer.

I did not react. I did not even smile. I couldn't. My body had frozen and my heart had stopped.

No. It was a joke. He was kidding. Or he was wrong. He read the wrong name. That had to be it.

"Claudia is an eighth-grader at Stoneybrook Middle School who likes art, reading mysteries, and fine dining . . ."

"Fine dining?" Kristy murmured.

"Aaaaaaaaaaagh!" I shrieked. "I won! I won!"

I jumped up and started falaping around the room.

Everyone else was staring at the radio as if it had suddenly grown horns.

"So, Claudia," the announcer went on, "if you're within the sound of my voice right now, please call five-five-five-WSTO. To repeat, that's — "

I was already on the W.

The phone rang on the other end — once, twice, three times.

I thought I would faint.

I caught Mary Anne's glance. She was grinning at me. Tears were forming in her eyes.

Finally I heard a male voice say, "WSTO, Radio Stoneybrook."

"Huck — heck — hum . . ."

Lovely. I'd won the contest of my dreams, and a frog had jumped down my throat.

"Excuse me, could you speak louder?" the voice asked.

"I'm Caudia Klishi!" I stammered.

"Yes, what can I do for you?"

"Claudia Kishi! I'm Claudia Kishi! I won the Host Contest!"

"Oh! Hey, congratulations! That was some essay!"

"Thanks."

"Listen, the station manager, Mr. Bullock, would like to tell you about the job in person. Say, tomorrow after school? Four-thirty or so?"

"Sure!"

He gave me directions. I grabbed the nearest pen and scribbled them down on a candy wrapper.

After blabbering a good-bye, I calmly, quietly hung up.

"Ya-hoooo!" Kristy whooped.

The room exploded. Mary Anne and Dawn threw their arms around me. Jessi and Mal jumped up and down, squealing.

"You're a star!" Dawn said.

"How come you didn't tell us you entered?" Kristy asked.

"I wanted it to be a surprise!" I explained.

For the rest of the meeting we talked about nothing else. I celebrated by digging out a box of Hostess chocolate cupcakes. (We almost forgot to call Mrs. Wilder back.)

I could not wait to tell my family the news.

CHAPTER 4

You know who's really, really great? My sister, Janine. I mean it.

Here's what happened when I broke the news at dinner: Mom and Dad smiled. Then Mom asked if the show would interfere with my schoolwork. Dad wanted to know if I would be paid.

Janine? She immediately ran into the kitchen. When she returned, she had a bottle of ginger ale and four wine glasses.

"A toast to Claudia, the first media celebrity in the family!" she announced.

"Hear, hear!" Dad said.

Janine was the first to clink glasses with me. She was wearing this huge grin.

I almost cried.

Between dinner and bedtime, every single BSC member called. Dawn gave me a list of songs to play (ecology-oriented, of course). Kristy told me her brother, Charlie, had agreed to drive me to the radio station the next day. Then she asked about seven hundred questions about the show. Shannon, Jessi, Mal, and Mary Anne each had questions of their own. I must have said "I don't know" a hundred times.

This distressed me. Was I *supposed* to know? Was Mr. Bullock really expecting me to come to the meeting with suggestions? Of course he was! I had written in my essay that I had good ideas flying around my brain. I had exaggerated. A lot.

Now what? Should I bring tapes to the interview? A list of talk-show-type topics? A list of people to interview? Or was this supposed to be a call-in show?

What had I gotten myself into?

That night I had nightmares. The entire world was listening to WSTO. Kids riding bikes and wearing headphones. Shoppers in malls. A capacity crowd in a sports arena with enormous speakers on stage, wailing: "And now, WSTO presents what you've all been waiting for — Claudia Kishi!"

And then, dead silence.

By morning I must have sweated off ten pounds.

I sleepwalked through school the next day. After last period, I walked to the front door, clutching my directions to the station.

Kristy was waiting for me there. Mary Anne and Dawn joined us soon after.

"Your barrette is crooked," Dawn said, reaching toward my hair.

"This is exciting," Mary Anne said, squeezing my hand.

"I'll go in with you if you want," Kristy volunteered.

"Uh, I don't think so, Kristy," I said.

"Hold still!" Dawn warned.

"Guys, it's not that big a deal!" I insisted.
HONK! HONK!

Saved by the Junk Bucket.

That's the name of Charlie Thomas's car, for exactly the kinds of reasons you'd expect. It is air-conditioned by two holes in the floor. You have to open the right front window with a monkey wrench. The rear floor is carpeted with crushed soda cans.

Kristy opened the back door, picked up an old T-shirt from the floor, and wiped off the seat. "Enter," she said.

"Good luck!" Mary Anne and Dawn shouted.

I climbed in back and Kristy got in front. "Thanks," I called out the window.

"I'll take good care of her," Kristy assured them. Then she yelled to a group of kids standing in front of the car: "Clear, please! Radio star coming through."

Bang! Clank! Rrrrroar! The Junk Bucket's noise was enough to scatter everybody.

We were off.

"Where to?" Charlie asked.

I read him the directions, and he clanked away from the school. His radio was turned up so loud, I expected the police to pull us over. The station? WSTO, of course.

"You ain't nothin' but a hound dog," sang the voice of Elvis Presley.

"Don't they play any *good* stuff?" Charlie asked.

"They will on *Claud's* show," Kristy replied confidently. "Right, Claud?"

"I guess," I said.

"Not to mention the guest appearances," Kristy barged on. "You will have kid guest appearances, right?"

"Well, I don't know."

"Or, like, a comedy hour," Charlie chimed in. "I memorized this Robin Williams routine and — "

"Hour?" Kristy shot back. "Don't be a hog, Charlie."

I sighed. Already this show was overwhelming me.

The radio station was on the outskirts of

Stoneybrook, in a low, tan brick building near the highway. Two tall towers stood next to it, with blinking lights on top. The Junk Bucket chugged noisily into the parking lot.

While Charlie waited in the car, Kristy walked inside with me to a small reception area. A young man sat at a desk, wearing a telephone headset and sipping coffee. His desk was piled with memos. On the walls around him hung photographs and plaques.

"Claudia?" he said, looking up.

"Yes," Kristy answered.

"Hi. My name's Max. I spoke to you on the phone — "

"I'm Kristy Thomas," Kristy said with a big grin, reaching out to shake the guy's hand.

He gave her a puzzled look. "You're the assistant?" he asked.

Kristy's eyes lit up. "Sure!"

"No!" I exclaimed.

All three of us laughed. I gave Kristy a sharp nudge in the ribs.

Max pressed a button on his telephone console and said, "The first-place girl is here, Mr. Bullock." Then he said to me, "He'll be out in a second. Have a seat."

Almost immediately a tall, thin, gray-haired man with glasses and a great smile walked into the room.

Kristy bounced to her feet.

"Claudia, this is Mr. Bullock," Max said.

Mr. Bullock energetically shook Kristy's hand. "Hello, there, Claudia! Congratulations!"

"Uh, Mr. Bullock," I said meekly, standing up. "*I'm* Claudia."

Mr. Bullock looked confused.

Ugh. What a great start.

I shot Kristy a Look. "This is my friend, Kristy. She'll be waiting outside to take me back."

"Great," Mr. Bullock said. He gave Kristy a friendly wink, then turned to me. "Okay, this way, Claudia."

I could feel Kristy's eyes burning a hole in the back of my head as Mr. Bullock led me down a hallway.

We passed three doors, marked *Studio* 1, *Studio* 2, and *Studio* 3. Through two of them I heard muffled sounds of music. The floors were thickly carpeted, and so were the walls (soundproofing, I guess). At the end of the hallway were two other doors, the one on the left marked *Conference Room* and the one on the right, *Station Manager*.

"My office," Mr. Bullock said, opening the door on the right. "Believe it or not, it's highly organized."

I tried not to laugh. The place was a pigsty. It looked sort of like my bedroom. I sat on a chair that was empty (probably just cleared for the occasion).

As Mr. Bullock began to close the door, I heard Max call out, "Mr. Bullock, the other girl's here."

Other girl?

"Terrific," Mr. Bullock said. "Send her in." He stood at the door, smiling. "Here's your assistant, Claudia."

"Assistant?"

Mr. Bullock nodded. "The second-place winner gets to assist you. Contest rules. And believe me, you'll be glad you have one. A radio show is hard work."

From my seat I could not see who was approaching. "Hello, there," Mr. Bullock said into the hallway. "Welcome to WSTO, and congratulations."

As my assistant walked through the doorway, I froze.

Ashley Wyeth was shaking hands with Mr. Bullock.

Ashley Wyeth, the Artist with a capital A. Ashley Wyeth, who moved to Stoneybrook from Chicago, where she had studied at the country's best art school. Who wore peasant dresses and combat boots and had six ear holes. Who liked my artwork and became my friend — then told me I should quit the BSC and devote my life to "my calling." Who almost single-handedly turned all my best friends against me.

Needless to say, Ashley and I did not remain friends. Not that we became enemies or anything (although the BSC members couldn't stand her). I just realized that an artist, especially a kid artist, had to have a life.

Ashley was the last person I'd have expected to see at WSTO. Why on earth had she entered *this* contest? Did she want old wax records to melt for a sculpture? Was she interested in sketching a microphone?

And why was she wearing normal clothes? Her outfit was a plain, button-down shirt and khaki slacks with running shoes. (She still had six studs in her ears, but I guess you can't plug up the holes, can you?)

"Claudia Kishi," Mr. Bullock said. "This is Ashley Wyeth."

Ashley smiled. "Hi, Claud. How's your art?"

"Great," I replied. "Yours?"

"Fine."

"So you know each other," Mr. Bullock said. "That's terrific."

I forced the sides of my mouth upward into a smile.

Mr. Bullock cleared off another chair, and Ashley and I sat. "Now, I want you to know how thrilled we are to have you two aboard," he said, sitting behind the desk. "As you know, your show will be twice weekly, Thursday and Saturday, for a month. The first show will be a week from this Thursday. You'll be planning and broadcasting the shows. How you two divide your duties is completely up to you. We've never done anything quite like this, so we'll be counting on you for ideas."

Gulp.

"Do you want a music show?" Ashley asked. "Or, like, call-ins and featured guests?"

"Yes." Mr. Bullock laughed. "In other words, anything goes. It's your show. We have facilities for all of the above. I'll just ask that you submit a program sheet the day of the first show, and at least a day in advance for subsequent shows. Remember, the station is at your disposal. And I've assigned one of our interns to help you. His name is Bob Atkinson, and he did a show like this in New York when he was a teenager. Okay?"

"Okay," I squeaked.

"Now, come on, let me show you around."

Mr. Bullock led us back into the hallway. He pushed open the incredibly thick, padded door to Studio 1. Outside the door was a red light that said *On Air*. It was unlit.

Inside was a room with electronic equipment crammed in every corner. Shelves of tapes and CDs lined the walls and a rock song was playing loudly.

One wall was glass, from about waist up. Through it I could see a man sitting at a desk. He was young and skinny, and his hair was in a ponytail. He was wearing earphones, bopping along with the song, and scribbling something on a sheet of paper.

"That's one of our engineers, testing the equipment," Mr. Bullock said with a smile. "You'll be sitting in this big room with your guests, and the tech staff will work behind the soundproof glass."

Wow. I was beginning to tingle. I could not wait to start.

Ashley was beaming, too.

The engineer caught a glimpse of us and waved his pencil. I waved back.

Mr. Bullock took us to a huge stockroom with nothing but shelves of records, tapes, and CDs. "Our library," he called it.

Next we saw the conference room. In there, a bearded, dark-blond-haired guy was putting labels on tapes while eating a donut.

"Bob, meet Claudia and Ashley," Mr. Bullock said.

"Heyyy, the two winners," he said, offering his hand. "Nice to meet you. Did Mr. Bullock manage to scare the daylights out of you yet?"

Ashley and I laughed. Neither one of us dared to say yes.

"Well, I'll leave you three," Mr. Bullock said. "Come talk to me if you have questions."

We said good-bye, and Bob pulled up a couple of folding chairs for us. I got three cups of water from a cooler in the corner. From under the piles of tapes, Bob pulled out a legal pad.

"Your first dangerous mission, should you accept it," he said, "will be finding two things: a title and a format. By format, I mean, how exactly are you going to divide up the hour? What kinds of features? How long? Will they be continuing? Varying from show to show? Stuff like that."

Nod, nod, nod, nodded Ashley and I.

"At some point, you'll want to look at these notes," he said, pushing the legal pad toward us. "Just some stuff I did in New York. Like . . . 'Mr. Science,' a call-in show on which kids learn weird science facts from this wise-cracking, street-smart character. Kids loved that. Then we had 'Book Talk.' Kids reviewed books and actually spoke to their favorite authors. You get the idea." He looked at his watch. "Now, I have a few things I need to do. Discuss amongst yourselves. I'll be back."

He rose from his seat, shot out the door, and closed it behind him.

I was alone in the room with Ashley Wyeth.

Suddenly I wished I had decided on the tuba, after all.

"I, uh, didn't know you were interested in radio," I said, trying to be friendly.

Ashley shrugged. "The contest sounded fun. It was sort of, you know, spur of the moment."

"But won't this take time away from your art?" I asked.

"I guess. But art isn't everything."

I laughed. "I never thought I'd hear *you* say that."

"Yeah. I guess not. Well, people change, huh?"

"Mm-hm. Sure. I guess."

Ashley pulled the legal pad close to her. "Okay, let's see . . ." she said. "We can definitely do without this 'Mr. Science' thing."

"Oh. I liked that idea."

"Are you serious?" She raised her eyebrows. "Well, you're the boss, aren't you?"

I did not like her tone of voice, but I let it pass. Instead I leaned over and read, " 'Tom the Taxi Driver' — special guest who answers kids' questions about feelings and behavioral issues." I burst out laughing. "Nahhh."

"Really? I think that sounds perfect," Ashley said.

Slowly but surely, my heart was starting to feel like the *Titanic*. Sinking fast.

CHAPTER 5

"How about 'For Kids Only,' " I suggested, taking a taco plate from the cafeteria display.

"I don't think we should have the word *kids* in the title." Ashley picked up a small sprouts salad, inspected it carefully, then finally put it on her lunch tray. "It's kind of patronizing."

Patronizing? You patronize *places*, right? Restaurants and stores? I had no idea what she was talking about.

" 'The Young Adults Education Hour'?" I suggested.

"Please."

" 'Yo, Dudes'?"

Ashley furrowed her brow. "It might be too informal."

"It was a joke, Ash."

I smiled. Ashley smiled. I grabbed two bowls of chocolate pudding and headed into the lunch room.

Have you ever met anyone with absolutely

no sense of humor? That's Ashley.

Our meeting at WSTO had been pretty much a disaster. We hadn't fought or anything. But we were in two different worlds. Immediately we'd forgotten Bob's instructions and started talking about features. Ashley would suggest something like "A Mozart Moment" or "Art Gallery Calendar," and I'd pretend to consider it. Then I'd come up with "Stoneybrook Top 40" or "Guest Movie Review," and she'd kind of snort and sniff and say, "Well, you're the boss."

So I had to humor her dumb ideas, and feel bad about mine.

Then Bob had returned to the conference room and reminded us to concentrate on a title and format. He'd suggested we meet him the next day with some "concrete ideas."

And here we were, the next day, and our concrete ideas were still in the mush stage.

" 'Something for Everyone,' " Ashley said as she sat at a table.

"Nice," I lied. "But that name could be for anything. Kids should hear the title and know what the show's about right away."

Ashley scowled and fed herself a mound of sprouts.

I didn't want to spend the whole day bickering about the title. So I decided to change the subject.

I pulled a pen and legal pad out of my shoulder bag and set them on the table. On the top page of the pad, in big letters, I had written *Format*? Underneath were notes I had taken.

"I was thinking," I said, "that maybe we should divide the show into three segments — "

"But what about a title?" Ashley insisted.

"We'll go back to that!"

"Okay. You're the — "

"What about making the first segment music?" I suggested. "That'll get us off to a good start."

Ashley frowned. "I don't know. You can hear music on any station. I was thinking of having a feature, like current events or something school-related."

Bo-ring! "What about a call-in segment?" I suggested.

Ashley thought about that for a moment. "Yeah, but you know some kids. They'll call up and act stupid."

"Yeah. The Alan Gray factor," I said. Alan once came to an art show of mine and put wadded-up gum all over the floor. He would definitely call the radio show just to burp — or something worse. Still, it might work.

"What about themes?" Ashley asked. "Like, a theme for each show? And all the segments can have something to do with it?"

A great idea from Ashley! I almost choked on my taco. "Uh-huh," I mumbled.

"We can play music related to the theme, interview people, maybe find some archival radio tapes."

Archival radio tapes? Puh-leeze. "Uh, why not just have kid guests. I mean, guests our own ages? You know, hold auditions, have people sing, read aloud, tell stories, whatever."

"Well, that could be part of it."

Now I could see Kristy and Mary Anne heading our way. Mary Anne was eyeing us with caution. Kristy was more obvious. She looked completely disgusted.

Ashley, as I mentioned, is not beloved by the BSC.

"Oh, *Ashley*," Kristy said, with the same tone of voice she might have used if she'd found Godzilla sitting next to me.

"Hi," Ashley replied.

"Ash is my assistant on the show," I quickly explained to Mary Anne. I had told Kristy about her on the way home from WSTO.

"You're doing an art show?" Mary Anne asked.

I carefully explained. I wanted to make sure Kristy and Mary Anne knew that Ashley wasn't up to her old tricks again.

I guess it worked. My friends sat with us and ate peacefully.

Well, at least Mary Anne did. Ashley and I had to put up with Kristy's constant questions. But by the end of lunch period, I had written down our tentative format:

FOUR KIDS ONLY (working titel)
1. Theams — one for each show, like: "Frenship," or something to do with a holiday or seasin, like that
2. 4 seggments of 15 minits each.
3. Possible segements :
   — Kid geusts, singing, telling storys, etc. etc. (to be picked by auditian
   — Interviews with kids book awthors if we can find some
   — Call-ins if posibile

When I finished, I passed it across to Ashley.

Kristy was still spilling out ideas. "Now, the play about baby-sitting will not only be educational, but a good advertisement for us — "

"Whoa, whoa," I said, "not so fast, Kristy. You're not on the show yet."

"I'm not?"

"Well, no. I mean, we haven't had auditions."

"Piece of cake," Kristy replied. "Mary Anne, you could play — "

"No," Mary Anne interrupted. "No way."

As Kristy rambled on, Ashley pulled a pen from her backpack.

"What's that for?" I asked.

"Your spelling," Ashley replied. "It's atrocious. And you also used the title we rejected."

I grabbed the sheet out of her hands. "It's only a rough draft, Ashley. And it says, '*Working* Title.' "

Ashley just shrugged. "Well, I guess you don't really need my help, then."

"What do you mean?"

"You and Kristy seem to have the whole thing worked out."

"You just called Claudia atrocious!" Kristy snapped.

"Not *her* — her spelling," Ashley replied.

"It's still not very nice," Mary Anne said quietly.

"Mm-hm. Okay. Well, ex*cuse* me." Ashley sniffed. "I was just trying to help."

"Yeah?" Kristy muttered. "Well, try a little harder next time."

"What?" Ashley said.

"Never mind."

Ugh. This was not getting any better.

I wasn't optimistic as Mrs. Wyeth drove us to WSTO after school. Ashley and I were just not hitting it off.

Bob was ready for us. He brought Ashley and me into the conference room and read my list (which I had typed and Spellchecked on the *Express* computer).

"Excellent!" was his first comment. (Yeaaaa!)

Next, he played some tapes of old shows he had worked on. In one of them, two kid hosts interviewed the author of a book called *I Hate English*, about a Chinese immigrant girl's trouble learning the English language. Then a panel of kids — some immigrants, some American-born — discussed the book. The show was incredible. I could have listened for hours.

Then we heard a call-in show about a book that some parents were trying to ban from a school library. Bob said that as a result of the show, the book was kept on the shelves.

A quiz show, book readings by guest actors, a comedy act . . . the tape was full of great stuff.

By the end of the tape I'd filled two pages with atrociously spelled notes.

"How do we get authors on the show?" I asked.

"Call or write their publishing company for information," Bob replied.

Scribble, scribble, scribble.

"What about auditions?" Ashley asked. "You know, for people our age?"

"We can put an ad in the *SMS Express*," I suggested.

"And we'll run periodic announcements on the air," Bob said. "You can hold the auditions in the studio. We'll set everything up. Just remember one thing."

"What's that?" I asked.

Bob laughed. "Don't book anything that'll cost us. Remember why you guys are here."

Ash and I looked at him blankly. "What do you mean?" I asked.

"Didn't Mr. Bullock tell you? About our financial state?"

Ash and I glanced at each other and shrugged. "Nope," she said.

"Well, one of our sponsors has backed out," Bob explained. "One that funded a lot of shows, including the show that's in your time slot. So . . . no sponsor, no money. The station had to fire a deejay and some of our staff. I'm amazed they kept me."

"The station's not going to close down or anything, is it?" I asked.

"Not yet. But it doesn't look too great."

"And that's why you had the contest?" Ashley said. "To get two unpaid staff members?"

"Well, I wouldn't put it so bluntly," Bob replied. "I mean, that was a consideration. But the station really believes in this concept. I believe in it. And I think you guys are going to be fantastic!"

After our meeting with Bob, Ash was furious. As we waited outside for her mom, I could practically see the storm clouds gathering over her head. "I can't believe they're using us like this," she grumbled.

"Oh, Ash, what's the difference?" I said. "We're doing this for the experience, right? We're going to run a radio show. Who cares about that other junk?"

Ashley grunted. I think she agreed with me. She just didn't want to admit it.

CHAPTER 6

Saturday

I'm sorry. I'm sorry. I'm sorry.

I tried to stop her, Claudia. Honestly I did. But it was no use.

Uh, excuse me, Dawn? I object!

What I meant to say, Kristy, was that your incredible creativity was so overwhelming at the Barrett/DeWitts today, that it made my head spin.

That's better.

Boy, was Kristy determined to be on my show. I'd only seen her like this once before, when she'd tried to convince a TV news team to interview the BSC members. (Why? Because the baby-sitting club *Dawn* had joined when she was in California had been on TV out there.)

Each day she seemed to have a new idea. On Wednesday she suggested running radio ads for the BSC (I'd open each show saying " 'For Kids Only,' sponsored by the Baby-sitters Club"!). Thursday she proposed a regular feature called "Thomas's Sitting Tips." Friday it was the "Krusher Scouting Report."

I figured she'd take a break over the weekend.

I was wrong.

On Saturday, Kristy and Dawn were scheduled to sit for the seven Barrett/DeWitt kids. (Four of them are from Mr. DeWitt's first marriage, and three of them from Mrs. Barrett's.) By the time Dawn arrived, Kristy was already setting two things on the picnic table in the backyard. One was a baby monitor (Marnie Barrett and Ryan DeWitt, who are both two, were napping in the bedroom they share.) The other thing was a cassette recorder.

"Hi!" Dawn said. "What's the machine for?"

"You'll see. You're in this, too."

Before Dawn could reply, Mr. and Mrs. DeWitt bustled out the back door and said their good-byes.

" 'Bye," yelled all the non-napping kids, who were playing freeze tag: Buddy Barrett and Lindsey DeWitt (who are eight), Taylor DeWitt (six), Suzi Barrett (five), and Madeleine DeWitt (four).

As the grown-ups headed toward their car, Kristy cupped her hands and called out: "Okay, how many of you guys want to audition for a radio show?"

"Meeeeee!"

Forget freeze tag. The five of them charged toward the picnic table.

Dawn rolled her eyes. "Claudia is going to kill you, Kristy."

Kristy laughed. "Nahh. Too many witnesses. Besides, we're just auditioning."

"Can I be the announcer?" Buddy cried out.

"No announcer," Kristy said. "This is a play, with parts for everybody."

"Yeaaaaaa!" the kids screamed.

"Can we do Robin Hood?" Taylor asked. "I'm Robin!"

"I'm the Sheriff!" Suzi called out.

"You're a *girl*," Buddy sneered.

"So?"

"So who am I supposed to play, Maid Marion?"

Lindsey shrieked with laughter. "Buddy's Maid Marion, Buddy's Maid Marion."

"Heyyyyy — "

Phweeet!

Kristy is the only girl I know who owns a referee's whistle. She takes it with her on baby-sitting jobs sometimes. It makes one of the loudest noises I have ever heard. I don't know why Marnie and Ryan didn't start shrieking from inside.

Outside, the kids quieted down.

"Okay, our show is called 'Tales of Baby-sitting,' " Kristy said. "We all play ourselves."

"Ourselves? That's no fun," Taylor complained.

"You just think so because you have the worst part in the show," Lindsey said.

"Hey!" Taylor protested.

"Be nice, guys," Kristy said. "We have to work together. Now, our first episode is called, 'A Messy Problem.' Dawn, you and I arrive at the house to see muddy footsteps on the carpet. You say, 'Hello, is anybody home? Oh, wow, Kristy, look at those footsteps.' Okay? Got that?"

Dawn laughed. "Kristy, I can't — "

"Say it," Kristy urged her.

"Um, hello is anybody — this is ridiculous — "

"Come on, Dawn," Kristy said. "Don't ruin the show."

"Yeah!" Buddy piped up.

"Oh-wow-look-at-those-footsteps," Dawn mumbled.

"Needs a little work, but not a bad start," Kristy said. "Now, Suzi, can you do a good scream?"

"*EEEEEEEEEEAAAAAGGHH!*"

The kids thought this was hysterical. They all started screaming, too.

Dawn claimed she lost some hearing in her left ear.

"Stop!" Kristy bellowed. "Now it's my line." She let out a fake-sounding gasp. Then, in a weird, overeager voice, "Oh, SUZI! What has HAPPENED? YOU have MUD all OVER your FACE, hands, and SHIRT!"

Suzi looked very concerned. "I *do*?"

"It's a play, dummy," Buddy taunted.

"I'm not a — "

"Now, Dawn, say, 'Gee, Suzi. What happened?' " Kristy directed.

"Why — I don't — oh, okay." Dawn repeated the words in a monotone.

Kristy turned to Suzi. "Now *you* say your brother was playing in the mud and he came inside and smeared you with it."

Suzi squealed with laughter. "Muddy

Buddy, muddy Buddy," she sang.

"Why am I the bad guy?" Buddy protested.

"*I'll* be the bad guy!" Taylor volunteered.

"Figures," Lindsey said.

"Guys . . ." Kristy warned.

"Oh, Kristy, what's the point?" Dawn asked.

Kristy exhaled with exasperation. "The point is for listeners to hear about effective baby-sitting techniques, but in story form. That makes it more interesting. And the tape is so we can listen to ourselves and fine-tune the acting. Okay?"

"Sure, Kristy," Dawn said.

"Now, my turn," Kristy barreled on. "Oh DEAR, Suzi, that is NOT acceptable BEHAVIOR, IS it? Oh, DAWN? Will you PLEASE go upSTAIRS and see where the OTHER children are and TELL them in a GENTLE but FIRM way that whoEVER brought the mud in must BEAR THE RESPONSIBILITY for cleanup? With our SUPERVISION, of COURSE.' "

"You've got to be joking," Dawn muttered.

Kristy slapped her hands rhythmically on the picnic table. "These'll be your footsteps going upstairs. Now, once you're up there, you see Buddy lying on his bed in a muddy outfit, and Taylor and Lindsey — "

"I'm not stupid enough to do *that*!" Buddy said.

"It's make-believe," Lindsey retorted.

"Do we use our real names?"

"Waaaaaaaaaahhhhhh!" squawked the baby monitor.

Dawn had never been so happy to hear a screaming toddler.

"It's Ryan. I'll go!" Dawn bolted from the table and flew inside. As she walked into the bedroom, Ryan was rubbing his eyes and whining. Marnie was still fast asleep.

"Hi, sweetheart," Dawn said, picking Ryan up. "Bad dream?"

Ryan nuzzled his face into Dawn's shoulder. She brought him into the kitchen. Through the window she heard Buddy's voice:

"Yes-you-are-right-Kristy-I-will-never-do-that-again." He sounded as if he were speaking English for the first time.

"THAT'S okay, Buddy. Heh heh. Kids will be kids," replied Kristy in her radio voice. "And did YOU get the MARKER stains off the WALL, Taylor?"

"Why are you talking so weird, Kristy?" Taylor asked.

Dawn couldn't help giggling. Ryan started giggling, too.

"Dawn?" Kristy called out.

Uh-oh.

"In here!" Dawn replied.

"Can you help us a little?"

With Ryan in one arm, Dawn trudged outside.

I was at Ash's house that afternoon, for a planning meeting. When I arrived home, my answering machine was flashing. The message was from Kristy:

"Claud. Guess what? I have the most fantastic idea for a regular feature. You will laugh your head off. It is so perfect. Call me soon so I can set up an audition. Otherwise, I may submit it to another station. Okay, 'bye."

Another station? *Please.*

Auditions were going to begin on Monday. I hoped desperately that Kristy's play was good.

CHAPTER 7

"A whole newwww worrrrrrld. . . ."

Ashley and I listened patiently as a little girl with braided hair sang meekly along with the soundtrack of *Aladdin*. Her mom sat a few feet behind her, grinning at us.

Ashley casually wrote something on the legal pad in front of her. She slid it to me and I read it.

HOW MANY TIMES HAVE WE HEARD THIS ?

Just as nonchalantly, I wrote

for.

Ashley looked puzzled. I realized I'd goofed, so I grabbed the sheet back and quickly wrote an *E* after the *R*.

It was Monday afternoon, about four-thirty.

We were sitting in the WSTO conference room, listening to auditions.

Lots of auditions.

The waiting room was packed with nervous kids and parents. Some had to wait outside in the parking lot.

They were lining up—for *my* show!

I felt like a Hollywood director.

How had we become so popular? The power of advertising. During the week, Ash and I had put up some fliers around town. Bob had announced the auditions regularly on the air, just as he'd said he would. By Friday, kids were stopping me in the school hallways to ask questions.

Bob had called me on Sunday to say that every single audition slot had been filled. That's one every six minutes, for an hour and a half on Monday and two and a half hours on Tuesday. *Forty* people were trying out. Plus, he had started a waiting list, which had grown to twelve names.

"You guys are the hottest thing in town!" Bob had said over the phone.

My response? Something like, "Eeeeeeeee!"

Then I'd called Ashley. She'd said, "Indeed? What pleasant news."

Just kidding. Her response had been more like, "Yahhh-hooooo!"

Yes, Ashley was loosening up. (Finally. Yeeeaaa!)

Monday passed in a blur. Ash and I met after school, and her mom drove us to the station.

That was when it really sank in. The parking lot was full. The waiting room was full. We had to weave through all the excited kids who were signing up. They whispered excitedly behind our backs as we passed.

We ran into the conference room and burst into giggles.

"Aaaaugh!" I screamed. "Can you believe this?"

Ash started doing some kind of Irish jig.

"Okay. Okay. Let's settle down," I said.

"Right." Ash took deep breaths. "Settle. Down."

Bob had set up a table and two chairs at the far end of the room. On it was a sheet with typed instructions:

Remember:
·Be fair. Keep All Auditions to the Allotted Six Minutes.
·Do Not Make Promises Yet. Tell Everyone You'll Call on Tuesday Night, After You've Made Your Decisions.
·Write Detailed Comments on Separate

Sheets. Suggestion: Rate Each Contestant 1 (Lowest) to 10 (Highest) and Compare Scores.

·*Keep Smiling!*

> *Best of Luck,*
> *Bob*

It was all stuff we'd discussed over the weekend. But I was glad he had typed it out. I was too nervous to remember any of it on my own.

"Ready and smiling," Ashley said, with this ridiculous, ear-to-ear grin.

I nearly cracked up. (I take back what I said about Ash's sense of humor.)

Soon Bob sent in auditioner number one, a girl named Lisa who started singing — you guessed it — "A Whole New World." In some unknown key. *Q,* maybe. Her face turned bright red every time she went for a high note. I stopped listening to the song and started worrying about her health.

Next, a pair of sixth-grade boys performed a comedy routine called, "Frank and Tim Visit Broadway." It went something like this:

Frank: Hey, want to see *Tommy?*
Tim: Who's Tommy?
Frank: Right.
Tim: Tommy Wright?

Frank: No, Who's Tommy!
Tim: That's what I asked you!
Frank: Never mind. How about *Cats*?
Tim: Oh, Tommy Katz! Why didn't you tell me?

And so on. You get the idea. Actually, it was pretty funny. I gave them a score of 8.

The third auditioner was a girl who could say anything backward instantly. She introduced herself as Nottus Haras (Sarah Sutton) and started pointing around the room, saying things like "enohporcim" and "tenibac elif." When I said "Wow, that's amazing," she replied, "Sknaht."

I liked her. (I hoped Yelhsa did too.)

Number four sang "A Whole New World." Unfortunately she sang it all on one note.

Seven-year-old Rosie Wilder, a BSC charge who has about a million different talents, played the coolest tune on the violin. It started out as classical, then turned into a medley of TV show themes. It was terrific, I thought.

So far, so good.

Then we heard our third "Whole New World," by Linny Papadakis, another of our charges. This was the loudest rendition so far. In fact, he kind of barked the lyrics. Out of the corner of my eye, I could see Ashley cringing.

On and on we went.

A chorus of little kids sang the theme song from "Shining Time Station." They were adorable.

We had three proposals for call-ins, all from SMS students: (1) "Bike Advice," by Pete Black and Erica Blumberg; (2) "Fashion Tips," by Sue Archer; and (3) "What's Happening This Weekend," by Cokie Mason.

And of course, the fourth "Whole New World"er, whom I mentioned before.

Near the very end, a boy with a skull mask walked in. In a husky voice, he introduced himself as Oswald McBelch and started burping on pitch (more or less) to "Row, Row, Row Your Boat."

I thought Ashley was going to have a cow.

"Alan Gray, is that you?" I demanded.

It was. Giggling hysterically, Alan ran out of the room, almost colliding with two frightened-looking girls in party dresses.

See what I mean? He is such a goon.

Despite Alan, we had a fantastic day. Tuesday started out well, too. We saw a kazoo band and a pair of girls named Julie and Jennifer who sang this hilarious song called "Friendship," which I'd once seen on an *I Love Lucy* show. A couple of other kids proposed a movie-review segment like *At the Movies*, and a trio of high school kids told ghost stories, complete with spooky sound effects.

Then Kristy arrived, with the Barrett/DeWitt kids.

Dawn, fortunately, had bailed out of the play by this time.

"Hi, Claudia!" Suzi and Taylor cried out, running through the door.

"We have a play!" Madeleine said.

"Duh," Buddy remarked.

Kristy was taking off her running shoes. "Okay, actors," she called out, "take your places!"

The kids wandered around, looking at the file cabinets and framed photos on the wall. Madeleine found the water cooler and was busy trying to work it.

"Here we go," Kristy went on. "Ahem. *A Messy Problem*, a play authored by Kristy Thomas."

With one running shoe in each hand, she pounded on the table top. "These are footsteps," she explained. Then she stopped pounding and called out, "HelLO, anybody HOME?"

No answer.

Knock knock knock! "Buddy," she whispered.

Buddy was reading the inscription on an

autographed photo. He spun around. "Oh! Uh, yeah. Come in. Claudia, who's the guy in the basketball uniform?"

"Bud*dyyyy*, the *play!*" Suzi said.

Buddy rolled his eyes. "Come *in*, Kristy!"

"OH my GOODNESS, LOOK at the muddy FOOTPRINTS on the CARPET!"

"AAAGGGGGH!" Suzi's scream almost made me lose my lunch.

Madeleine choked on her cup of water. She began coughing and sputtering. Ashley and I bolted up from the table and ran to her.

The door flew open. Mr. Bullock rushed in and asked, "Is everything all right?"

"Fine, fine," said Kristy. "It's part of my play."

"Oh. Sorry." Mr. Bullock ducked out.

Well, I don't need to go into the gruesome details, except to say that Madeleine recovered but refused to participate, Buddy kept looking at the pictures, Taylor "went up" on one of his lines and burst into tears, and Kristy insisted on pounding her sneakers on the table every time someone in the play needed to walk.

By the end of six minutes, clumps of dried dirt were sprinkled all over the table, Kristy was scolding Buddy, and the play itself had barely started.

"Uh, Kristy," I said politely. "Time's up."

I expected her to argue, but she didn't. Instead she said, "Well, you get the main idea, Claud. What time will we be on?"

Ashley and I exchanged a look. "Uh, we're notifying everybody tonight," I said.

"One way or the other," Ashley added.

Kristy nodded solemnly. "Right. I guess you have to say that, huh? Okay, see you. Come on, guys!"

Sneakers in hand, she padded out of the office, with the five Barrett/DeWitts behind her, all shouting good-bye.

That evening, Ashley and I met in my room. I broke out a bag of caramel-flavored popcorn rice cakes and a box of Oreos. We spread out our audition notes on the bed.

"Okay," I said. "The first 'Whole New World' girl?"

"Very shy." Ashley sighed. "You know, I think this rating system is so . . . dehumanizing."

"I gave her a two," I said.

"Me, too."

"How about 'Frank and Tim Visit Broadway'?" I asked. "I thought they were funny."

Ashley rolled her eyes. "Bo-ring. Another two."

"I liked them. I said eight."

"Well, you're the boss."

Why did she have to say that?

"Um, how about Sarah the backward talker?" I asked.

"Weird kid," Ashley said. "I can see how that would appeal to a mass audience, but I said three. You can't seriously think . . ."

I showed her the 10 I'd written on my sheet.

"No way!" Ashley said.

I thought for a moment. "Yaw!" I replied.

Ashley looked at me blankly.

"*Way*, backward?" I said.

"Oh. Ha ha."

Well, by the time we had finished, we'd disagreed on about half the performers. One that we agreed on a hundred percent was Kristy.

The play was out.

And guess who had to tell her?

CHAPTER 8

"You *what*?"

I knew Kristy wasn't going to take rejection lightly. She was the last person I called Tuesday night.

"Kristy," I explained patiently, "we felt the play would be a little too long, and — "

"It's exactly fifteen minutes."

"Uh-huh. But — "

"If you want, we can cut it. No problem."

"It's just that, well, some of the kids don't seem . . . ready."

Kristy took a deep breath. "Yeah. I guess they were a little rambunctious. But you are going to have more auditions, right?"

"Sure. We haven't filled up the whole month."

"All *riiight*. 'Bye."

I could practically hear her mind working. I knew we hadn't heard the last of Kristy Thomas.

* * *

Now for the hard part.

We'd accepted about ten acts. But we could only use four of them in the first show. Plus we needed to choose a theme.

(We should have chosen the theme first. That would have made it easier to pick the acts. Of course, we hadn't thought of that.)

On Wednesday Ashley walked home with me from school. Before the BSC members arrived, we'd have time for a planning session.

Over snacks, of course. No sense starving while you're planning.

Ashley crunched away on some Doritos. I, meanwhile, was savoring a Chunky.

"So how do we do this theme thing?" I asked.

Ashley swallowed before speaking. " 'Do this . . . theme thing'?" she repeated, as if I'd just said something in baby talk.

"Yeah. Like, let's say we pick a theme. You know, fashion, or art. How do we fit in Sarah the backward talker?"

"Well," Ashley said with a smile, "*I* wasn't the one who wanted to use her."

Ooh, I wanted to slap Ashley. But I didn't. I was calm and cool. She was my assistant. She didn't have to be my best friend.

"Friendship," I said. It was the first word

that popped into my mind. "Like the song Julie and Jennifer sang. How about that for a theme?"

Ashley frowned. "Well, it was only one song."

"I know. But we could, like, build the show around the song. You know, have the guests talk about what friendship means to them."

"I don't know — "

"No solo acts for this show — just twos and threes. Then they can talk about their friend-ships."

"How it affects their artistry."

"Exactly." (In Ashley-esque terms.)

Ashley shrugged and gave me a *well, you're the boss* look.

You know what? I didn't care. I *was* the boss. And it was a good idea.

I popped another Chunky in my mouth, grabbed a pen, and looked at the list of acts we had accepted. I circled these:

Frank and Jim (comidy)
Peet and Ericka (Bike advise)
Shinning Time stacion carrus
Bil and Katie (at the movys)
Rijena, Cathy, David (goeat storys)

"See?" I said. "All of these guys seemed like great friends. Let's choose three. We'll call them to discuss the theme. Then we'll put the friendship song last."

"One problem. The song isn't anywhere near fifteen minutes long."

"Well . . . we'll ask the girls to sing more than one song. There are plenty more songs based on friendship, right?"

" 'Ben,' " Ashley replied.

"Ben who?" I asked.

"The song 'Ben.' About the boy and the rat."

"Yuck."

"It's beautiful. It goes like this: 'Bennnnn . . .' "

Guess what? Ashley may be a great artist, but her singing is as bad as my spelling.

"Aaaugh, stop!" I said. "You'll break my windows!"

Ashley's face turned red. We both cracked up.

Well, by the end of our meeting, we'd decided on our big three: the comedy act, the kiddie chorus, and the movie reviewers.

Ashley left at quarter after five. I had fifteen minutes until the BSC meeting.

I picked up the phone. My first call was to Frank (of Frank and Tim). He was delighted — until I mentioned the friendship angle.

"There's one problem," he said softly. "I hate Tim."

"Oh, but I'm sure you can — "

"*Rank!* See, now *that* is comedy!"

Ugh. Maybe Ashley was right about these guys.

For the kids' chorus, I called Ms. Farrell, one of the moms who brought the group to the radio station. She thought the theme was a great idea, because *Shining Time Station* is all about friendship and cooperation.

Bill Shebar, the movie reviewer, seemed a little embarrassed about the theme. But he agreed to call his partner, Katie Geissinger, to discuss it.

Last, I called the two girls who sang "Friendship," Julie Mansfield and Jennifer Evans. They said they'd try to find two or three more songs to sing.

Whew. This was turning out to be a lot of work. But I was doing it. Me, Claudia Kishi. The artist. The girl who thinks *planning* means buying Twinkies ahead of time.

You know what? I was pretty proud of myself.

I could not wait until showtime.

I was out to lunch during school on Thursday. Afterward I put together this great new outfit and trimmed my hair.

I know. Double duh. It was a radio show. Nobody was going to see me. But I could not help it. Honestly. I absolutely had to do it. I don't know why.

Anyway, I wore the coolest tuxedo I'd recently bought in a thrift shop, including a silky, piped shirt and a bright red velvet cummerbund. I removed the shoulder pads from the jacket, which made it really slouchy (I love that look). Then I bought a pair of white socks with silver glitter.

I decided to wear a pair of red sneakers to match the cummerbund. I swept my hair up and fastened it with a rhinestone barrette in the shape of a musical note.

Last, I carefully folded up a speech I had written, typed, and Spellchecked on the *SMS Express* computer. I put it in the inner pocket of my tux jacket.

My dad left work early so he could drive me to the station, with WSTO turned up almost to full volume. He kept nodding his head and saying, "Nice station," even though we only heard the weather, the sports, and a few ads.

He was grinning ear to ear when he dropped me off. "Good luck, sweetheart. We're proud of you," he said.

My dad hardly ever says that (to me, at least). I nearly lost it. Boy, was I glad I'm not Mary Anne. "Thanks, Dad," I replied. "Don't forget to tape it."

"I bought fresh batteries," he called out as he drove away.

Ashley was already in the studio when I walked in, dressed in jeans and a workshirt. She was deep in conversation with Bob, but when she saw me, she howled with laughter.

"Are you going to, like, describe your outfit to the listeners or something?" she asked.

"Ha ha," I replied. "Nice to see you, too."

I tried to look mean. At least serious. But Ashley's face looked like Christmas morning.

I let out a scream. She let out a scream. We hugged each other. We jumped up and down.

"Uh . . . harrumph," Bob said.

"Oh. Right. The show." I could barely speak, I was grinning so hard.

We gave Bob our program sheet. Somehow we managed to discuss it with him and Mr. Bullock. One by one, the guests started filtering into the waiting room next to the studio. I think I said hi, but I don't remember. I was sooo nervous.

An engineer knocked on the window and pointed to the clock. It was 4:56, and the show began at 5:00.

Yikes!

Ashley and I put on our earphones (unfortunately, that meant taking off my barrette).

Mr. Bullock rushed in and wished us good luck. Bob gave us a salute and sat in a corner to watch. An engineer's voice began calling out, "Ten . . . nine . . . eight . . ."

I grabbed Ashley's hand, which was clammy. She was shaking. I was shaking.

". . . Six . . . five . . ."

And I realized my speech was still in my pocket.

I let go of Ashley. I reached into my jacket with my right hand.

Wrong side. My finger caught in a rip in the lining.

". . . three . . . two . . ."

My left hand jabbed my chest. My fingers fluttered and fumbled. I had no control. My brain was somewhere in the Limbo Zone.

A red light blinked on above my head.

"You're on the air!" the voice said over the headphones.

Gulp.

The speech. It was in my hand. I had it. I smoothed it out on the table.

I could not understand a word.

"It's upside down!" Ashley whispered.

On the other side of the soundproof glass, an engineer started cracking up.

He had heard Ashley!

Quickly I turned the speech around. "Heek kew."

Oh. Oh. This was not happening. My throat was dry as dust.

I quickly swallowed. Ashley's eyes looked like white Frisbees.

"Hello and welcome to 'For Kids Only'!"

I did it! I took a deep breath and went on. "This is Claudia Kishi, coming to you live from the WSTO studios, along with Ashley Wyeth, and this is our first show. Today our theme is *friendship*."

As I continued speaking, Ashley's Frisbees slowly shrank. When I finished my speech, her eyes were more or less normal-sized.

Frank and Tim performed their comedy act. But they added a new section about being friends. It consisted mostly of dumb insults, such as "With friends like you, who needs parents?" and "Tim's a great buddy. I lend him my math homework and he lets me copy his lunch."

Next the kids sang. Afterward we asked them about the train characters of *Shining Time Station*, and then about their own experiences. They were very talkative. One little boy chattered about a pen pal in Japan. "I'm saving up to go visit him and I already have six dollars and twenty cents!" he announced.

Bill and Katie, the movie reviewers, talked about movies that featured strong friendships (great idea, huh?).

The only problem was that everybody was going too fast. I tried desperately to stretch out my introductions, and that helped a little.

Julie and Jennifer began their song at five forty-two, three minutes early. (Do you know how long three minutes is, in radio time? *Forever*.)

Ashley and I both signaled them to take their time (which was kind of useless, since they were singing to tapes).

First they sang the buzzards' song from the movie *The Jungle Book*. Then a pop song, "That's What Friends Are For." And finally, the song from *I Love Lucy* (which they said was written by a guy named Cole Porter). My absolute favorite line went like this:

"When other friendships have been forgot,
ours will still be hot!"

They finished at five fifty-nine.

One minute left.

I looked at Ashley. Her face looked like a human question mark.

The engineer was signaling me to go on.

Dead air. That's radio talk for silence. You're not supposed to let it happen for more than a second or two.

"Um," I said. "Thank you all for listening.

This is Claudia Kishi and Ashley Wyeth, with 'For Kids Only.' This has been our first show. We hope you tune in Saturday."

Forty-three seconds were still left.

Ashley nudged me. I shrugged. That was all I'd planned to say.

You know what I was thinking?

What would Stacey do in a situation like this?

Stacey is about the coolest person I know. She'd know how to handle dead air. She'd just say what was on her mind.

I took a deep breath. "And, uh, most of all, I hope you enjoyed our . . . *theme* today," I said. "Friends are really important, you know. They're like a special gift. A second family. I guess I'm pretty lucky, because I have lots of friends, and they all live in Stoneybrook. I used to have a best friend, too, but not anymore. I — I really miss her."

Boy, it felt weird admitting that over the air. But it was true.

"Anyway," I continued, "maybe she's listening right now. And if she is, I hope she liked the show."

I looked at the clock. Ten seconds left.

"So . . . we'll see you Saturday, and don't forget: If you'd like to audition for 'For Kids Only,' just call the station at 555-WSTO. That's all the time we have now. Good night."

Above my head, the red light went off. Bob was beaming. "I am *soooo* proud of you," he said.

I screamed. Ashley screamed. Frank and Tim did a routine of strange high-fives. Bill, Katie, Julie, Jennifer, and the kids were all hugging like crazy.

We mobbed Bob. He shouted for help, but no one listened.

Mr. Bullock walked in with a huge smile. He laughed and laughed.

Me? I had only one regret.

I had brought absolutely no junk food in my backpack.

Saturday

Today Kristy and I sat for my brothers
and sisters. Everything went well, except
I have a question for Claudia.
   You're not planning to extend this
radio show past one month, are you?

Can you guess why Mallory asked that question? If you think it has something to do with Kristy, you're right.

It also has to do with the Oogly Oogly Beast.

Oogly had become very popular in the Pike house. That Saturday, Claire and Margo had begged Mallory to tell them another story.

Mallory was in the middle of one when Kristy arrived.

"Hi, everyone!" Kristy called out, bounding into the den.

Claire glared at her. "Sssshhh!"

"Hi, Kristy!" Mallory said. "The boys are outside with Vanessa."

"Come *on*. Finish the *story*," Claire whined.

"Don't be rude," Margo warned her.

"Pleeeeease," Claire said, rolling her eyes.

Kristy headed out of the room, toward the backyard.

" 'Who's been eating my dinner?' roared the Oogly Oogly Beast," Mallory said. "Rusty-locks slowly peeked out from behind the entertainment center. 'I did,' she squeaked. Well, the Oogly Oogly Beast's eyes bugged out. The hairs on his shoulders stood on end. Smoke poured from his ears. He gritted his teeth, flexed his claws, and stomped toward Rusty-locks. 'Rrrrrragggh! You must pay for this terrible crime!' he growled. 'But what did I do?'

Rustylocks asked. The Beast just roared again and drew his snarling face up to hers.''

Mallory paused. She let Claire and Margo sit there for a moment, frozen, their mouths hanging open.

'' 'Yoooouuu,' the Oogly snarled. 'Yooouuu neglected to put the plate into the dishwasher. Goodness me, I will simply *not* tolerate messy housekeeping!' ''

Margo and Claire fell off the sofa, laughing.

And Kristy reappeared in the doorway.

"Mallory, it's perfect," she said.

"Thank you," Mal replied with a modest smile. "I — I just made it up."

"You should write it down. Really. Take my word. It'll help."

"Help what?"

"For the audition. I think that was my problem. See, the Barrett and DeWitt kids are too young to read, but *your* brothers and sisters can."

"Except Claire," Margo piped up.

"Can *too*!" Claire retorted. "I know all the letters!"

"Whoa, hold it," Mallory said. "No, Kristy. The answer is no. I can't audition in front of all those people."

"You were great, Mal!" Kristy said. "You're a natural performer."

"Telling stories at home is easy. No way am I going to go on the radio!"

(Mallory, as you can guess, is a little shy.)

Kristy sat on the arm of the sofa. She looked away, thinking. "Well, what if *I* do it, then?"

"No!" Claire cried. "You can't do it like Mallory."

"How does he speak?" Kristy scrunched up her face and used a nasal voice. " 'Uh, excuse me, but this floor is dirty.' Like that?"

Margo giggled. "You sound so dorky."

"Thank you," Kristy replied in her Oogly voice.

"Not so exaggerated," Mallory said. "Just pretend to be a really fussy person."

Mallory trained Kristy for awhile. Kristy wasn't getting the voice properly, but that didn't seem to matter to her.

Kristy borrowed a notepad and pen from Mal, then ran into the yard. Mal, Claire, and Margo followed closely behind her.

"Who wants to try out for Claudia's show?" Kristy called.

"Meeee!"

Round two was about to begin. This time, without a tape recorder.

Kristy sat on the grass as all seven of Mal's siblings gathered around her. "Buddy told me you already tried out," Nicky said, "and Claudia said no."

"Well, this'll be different," Kristy insisted. "She will crack up. We're going to do an Oogly Oogly Beast story."

"All *riiiight!*" Jordan said.

"Okay," Kristy barged on, "let's say, the Oogly goes to . . ."

"Disney World!" Vanessa suggested.

"A baseball game!" Adam said.

"The bathroom!" Nicky cried.

Margo groaned. "*Gross*, Nicky!"

"How about this?" Kristy said. "The Oogly Oogly Beast goes to Stoneybrook Elementary School?"

"And eats my teacher!" Byron added.

Claire sneered. "Eww. Too messy."

Kristy began writing. She recited each word she wrote. "This . . . is . . . the . . .story . . . of . . . a . . . very . . . neat . . . monster." She laughed. "Oh, that's a good one. A neat monster. Get it?"

Mallory cringed. "Uh, Kristy?"

Kristy just barged on. "The . . . monster's . . . name . . . was . . . the . . . Oogly . . . Oogly . . . Beast . . . and . . . he . . . loved . . . to . . . be . . . clean."

After a few minutes of this, Mallory had to go back inside. She couldn't take it any more.

Suddenly her great creation — her very own character — seemed kind of stupid.

As she wandered into her room, she could hear her siblings laughing like crazy outside.

As for me, well, I felt as if my life had been taken over by the show. (Surprised?) On Saturday night, our second one had been a little rocky. The theme had been "Family." I talked about my family, but when I mentioned Peaches and Mimi, I choked up. I almost blew my nose into the mike (*very* cool). Then our first act, a brother and sister, arrived ten minutes late because they'd had a fight. I had to switch acts around, and everyone became nervous and began flubbing lines. And I kept speaking too close to the mike, so every time I said a word with the letter *P* I caused a small explosion.

Plus a couple of our future guests had called to cancel, so we needed to hold more auditions soon.

But the good news was that WSTO had already received some mail and calls about the show — all raves!

Mom and Dad had promised to take Janine and me out for dinner on Saturday evening. As usual, I was late getting dressed. Mom had already called me twice from downstairs. I could hear the car starting in the driveway.

Rrrrrring!

Oh, great. Of all times for a phone call.

I thought about letting the answering machine take the call. But I didn't do it. Quickly I picked up the receiver. "Hello?"

"Claudia, it's me, Kristy."

"Oh, hi. Listen, I need to — "

"I think I've got it!"

"Got what?"

"An act. A great one. When can we audition?"

My heart sank.

I should have let the machine answer it.

CHAPTER 10

"Knock, knock," said Jackie Rodowsky.

"Who's there?" I asked.

"Lena."

"Lena who?"

Jackie grinned. "Lena little closer and I'll tell you!"

Hahahahahahahahaha!

That was a laugh track. Bob was sitting with us in the conference room and fooling around with sound equipment.

We were halfway through our Tuesday auditions. The turnout was even bigger than last time, but the talent wasn't as good. (Bob said that when a show becomes popular, everybody wants to hop aboard.)

Jackie was giggling so hard at the laugh track, he could barely deliver the next joke.

"Knock knock," he finally said.

"Who's there?" Ashley, Bob, and I all asked.

"Hatch."

"Hatch who?"

"Gesundheit!"

Hoo hoo hee hee ho ho ho!

Bob was now playing a recording of one man bellowing with laughter. Well, Jackie laughed so hard at that, he fell off his chair.

He grabbed onto the table on his way down. Unfortunately, Ashley's and my half-filled plastic water cups were on it.

The table tipped and wobbled. Cups, papers, and pens went flying off the end.

"Whoa!" Ashley yelled.

Bob bolted out of his seat to help Jackie, who had been bopped by a flying cup. "Are you okay?" he asked.

His face was red and his hair was wet. "Oops," was all he said.

"It's my fault," Bob said. "Those laugh tracks are too distracting."

It wasn't his fault. He just doesn't know Jackie. "The Walking Disaster" is how the BSC members refer to him. Falling and spilling are two of his greatest talents. I keep hoping he'll grow out of it, but he hasn't yet.

After Ash and I helped clean Jackie up, Bob thanked him for the audition and guided him safely back to the waiting room.

I sat down again and gathered my notes. Next to Jackie's name I wrote, *Cute, but where to fit?*

Ash and I had become much smarter about these auditions. We had decided on the themes for our next three shows in advance — "It Ain't Easy Being a Kid," "My Favorite Place in the World," and "What Are You Reading?"

"Guys, we have a return customer!" Bob announced as he entered the room again.

Behind him was Kristy, clutching a few stapled-together sheets of white paper.

And behind her, also holding sheets, trudged Adam, Jordan, Byron, Vanessa, Nicky, Margo, and Claire Pike.

"Claudia-silly-billy-goo-goo!" Claire called out.

"Hello, everybody, we are the Thomas-Pike players!" Kristy announced.

"Pike-Thomas," I heard Byron mutter.

Kristy read from the papers: " 'Today we present the story of a very . . . *neat* monster.' " She looked at each of us and grinned, as if she'd told a joke.

Then Jordan began reading in a mumble so low I could barely hear him. " 'The monna nimwa Oogelbee and he luvva be clean.' "

"Speak up!" Kristy whispered.

But before Jordan could repeat it, Vanessa shouted, " 'EVERY TIME HE DID SOME-THING SCARY, HE WAS JUST UPSET ABOUT THE MESS.' "

Margo held up her sheet in front of her face. " 'Like . . . the time . . .when he . . . um, arrived home . . . and he . . . he saw Rr . . . Rrroo style — ' "

"Rustylocks, you dummy!" Nicky hissed.

Margo stuck out her tongue. " 'Rusty-locks,' " she continued. " 'And . . . he — ' "

"Hey! My turn!" Adam said. " 'And he said, "You ate my food but you didn't put the plate in the dishwasher." ' "

Kristy laughed. "Great, Adam!"

Ashley gave me a sideways glance. She had this tense, little smile on her face.

Bob looked totally bewildered.

And I knew I was going to be making another painful phone call.

After the auditions, Ashley and I carefully pored over our lists.

"I liked the kid who knew sports trivia," I said.

Ashley made a face. "I hate sports."

"I do, too. But I think kids will like him."

"Well, that's probably true."

"A keeper?"

"Yup. How about Jackie?"

I just gave her a Look.

She sighed. "Yeah, I feel the same way."

You know what? Ashley was improving. Either that or I was being more tolerant. Whatever. The thing is, I didn't feel like strangling her every two seconds.

Maybe every two *minutes*. (Just kidding.)

A moment later Bob poked his head in the room. "You guys hungry? I'm on my way to the snack machine to get a Milky Way or something."

I reached into my shoulder bag. "Is a Snickers okay?"

"Sure. But what about you?"

"I have more." I tossed him the Snickers and began rummaging through my bag. "Milk Duds, Peppermint Patties, and I think a box of Raisinets."

Ashley laughed. "What, no Heath bar?"

"Ohhhh, sorry," I said. "I ate it on the way over."

"Man, I would love to be your dentist," Bob remarked, biting into the Snickers bar. He plopped himself into his chair. "Maybe that's what I should do, become a dental assistant."

"Right," Ashley said.

"I'm serious. I may need the work soon, the way things are going here."

"Uh-oh," I said. "Are they going to fire you?"

Bob shrugged. "You know what they say: 'Last one hired, first one fired.' Mr. Bullock tries to be positive about it all, but he's been dropping hints."

"What'll you do?" Ashley asked.

"I don't know. I'm only paid a small stipend here, but I really need it. It goes right to my tuition. Maybe I'll leave college for awhile."

I didn't know what to say. Neither did Ashley. He looked so sad.

Over Bob's shoulder, I noticed that the clock read 6:27. My dad was supposed to pick up Ashley and me at six-thirty. "Um, we have to go," I said.

"I'll walk you to the parking lot," Bob volunteered.

We gathered our stuff and began heading down the hall toward the front door.

"I just can't imagine Stoneybrook without WSTO," I said. "I remember listening to it when I was a kid."

Bob nodded. "Me, too. And my parents heard the end of World War Two announced on WSTO when *they* were kids. Our listeners are going to be shocked big-time if the station goes down the drain."

"Don't they know about it?" Ashley asked.

"Nahhh," Bob replied. "The station policy has been to keep it quiet. If our advertisers find out, they'll want to desert us. No one wants to stay aboard a sinking ship."

I waved to Max and pushed the front door open. "That's dumb. If you get more people to listen, then the advertisers will want to put ads in the show. Right?"

"Yup," Bob said, holding the door for Ashley.

"So let everybody know," I went on. "The listeners care about the station. Maybe they can write to advertisers. Or donate money. Like an emergency fund."

"True," Bob said. "I mean, it's not the way things are done in commercial radio, but — "

"I think it's unfair not to tell the listeners," Ashley remarked.

"I suppose I could broadcast an editorial," Bob said. "But I'd have to get Mr. Bullock's permission."

"Write an article for the *Stoneybrook News*, too," I suggested. "That way you might reach some new listeners."

Honk! Honk!

Dad was parked in a spot at the other end of the lot. He waved at us.

"You guys better go," Bob said. "Good work."

"Will you talk to Mr. Bullock about all this?" Ashley asked.

"Sure, sure," Bob replied. "Hope springs eternal, huh?"

He smiled as we headed toward the car.

But judging from the look on his face, hope was the furthest thing from his mind.

CHAPTER 11

"You *what*?"

I could not believe it. Our Thursday show was about to begin. I was in the studio, setting up with Ashley, Bob, Mr. Bullock, and the engineers. And now one of our guests, Peter Hayes, was calling up to cancel.

Peter is a great athlete. He has set a bunch of middle-school track records. For our theme, "It Ain't Easy Being a Kid," he was going to talk about sports pressure at the state level.

"I twisted my ankle," Peter said. "I was skateboarding."

"And you can't walk?"

"Claudia, I have to go to the doctor. Now. I mean, come *on*, I didn't do this on purpose!"

I inhaled and counted to three. Then I exhaled and said, "I know. Sorry, Pete. Good luck. I hope you feel better."

"Thanks, Claud."

"No problem." I was courteous. I was polite. I was compassionate.

And then I hung up.

"He's a track star, and he twisted his ankle on a skateboard!" I exploded. *"Arrrrgh!"*

"What do we do now?" Ashley asked.

"Can you do a good imitation of a track star?" Bob asked.

"Very funny," I said, pacing the floor. "How on earth are we going to fill fifteen minutes?"

"Music?" Ashley suggested.

"We can't forget the theme," I reminded her.

"Talk about the pressures of the Baby-sitters Club," Ashley suggested.

"Kristy would kill me," I said. "She'd think it was bad publicity."

The room fell silent. I could hear the equipment buzzing. The clock said 4:50. Ten minutes to showtime.

My mind was flying.

"It Ain't Easy Being a Kid." I sure knew enough about that subject. From my home life, from my friendships, from my personals column.

That would be perfect. A personals column on the air. Well, not personals, exactly. But complaints and advice, more like Dear Abby.

"Okay, let's do a call-in," I said. "Advice for kids."

"From us?" Ashley asked.

"Why not? We can try."

"Peer counseling," Mr. Bullock said. "Good idea. I say go for it."

Ashley didn't look convinced. But she agreed. And that was all that mattered.

Rosie Wilder was the guest on our first segment. She played her funny violin piece, then talked with me on-air about her conflicts. The fifteen minutes went by super-fast.

In our next two segments, we interviewed some of Ash's SMS friends she'd invited to be on the show: identical twins, and then a boy who had lived in six different places (in three countries) over the past five years.

Throughout the show, I kept saying, "And remember, our 'For Kids Only' call-in begins at five-forty-five. Tell us what's on your mind."

An engineer had set up a huge telephone near me, with six lines. By 5:44, all six were lit up.

Ashley was sweating. She squeezed my left hand. I could feel my throat tightening. I picked up the phone and said, " 'For Kids Only.' You're on the air."

"Hi, Claudia?"

"Yes?" I said. "Who am I speaking to?"

"Um, my name's Joanne. I really love your show, and I just wanted to ask you something. I had this argument with a friend, and I told her I never wanted to speak to her. But now I realize I was stupid. She hates me, but I want to be her friend again. What do I do?"

"How do you know she hates you?" I asked.

"She doesn't talk to me in school anymore."

"Has either of you called to apologize?"

"No."

"Well, someone has to do it. Why not you? Just tell her exactly what you told me."

"But she'll hang up on me!"

"I don't believe that, Joanne. I think you need to try. I bet she'll stop being mad."

"You think?"

"Yup. And good luck, Joanne."

Ashley gave me a thumbs-up.

Why, *why* did that call make me think of Stacey?

The next caller wanted to complain about a teacher. Ashley handled that one.

Caller three was a girl named Cheryl who asked, "When you're baby-sitting, how do you deal with a one-and-a-half-year-old boy who won't go to sleep?"

Right up my alley. "First try singing to him. If that doesn't work, pick him up and pace back and forth — but keep singing. If he still won't sleep, try some warm milk with a little honey in it. If you have a rocking chair, sit in it and rock back and forth while telling a long story. . . ."

I went through every baby-sitting trick in the book. Cheryl listened carefully and thanked me.

The next caller blurted out, "Why do kids have to do homework? It's the stupidest thing in the world!"

"Do you need some help with your homework?" Ashley asked.

Nah. He'd already done it. It turned out he just wanted to complain.

I answered a few calls. Ashley answered a few. Together we managed to give advice about hair, clothes, boys, girls, parents, grandparents, teachers, you name it. The time was racing by.

At 5:58, I announced, "Okay, I think this'll be our last call. Hello, you're on the air."

Sniff. Sniff. "Hello?"

When I heard the sniffling, I immediately thought Mary Anne was calling. But the voice was different.

"Hi. This is Claudia."

"Hi." *Sniff.* "Um, my name's George Hewitt. I'm eleven. And . . . and my parents are, well, it's like, they hate each other. They always fight. Now my dad hasn't been home for a few days, and my mom says they're going to get a divorce."

I could see Ashley turning about three shades of pale. (I wasn't feeling too comfy myself. I'd sort of been hoping for a discussion about clothes or videos.)

"You sound very upset," I said.

"Well," George went on, "my mom got really angry today, and she started screaming at my little sister, Rachel. And Rachel started saying how she wished Mom would go away and Dad would come back. Then Mom started crying, and Rachel said . . . well, she said Mom should die, and both of them ran to their rooms. I tried to talk to them, but they told me to go away. I don't know, I guess — I guess I just feel helpless. What should I do?"

Whew. How were we going to handle this? I looked at Ashley, but she just shook her head.

I thought about my personals column. Back then, a boy had written me with a similar problem. I referred him to a therapist named Dr. Reese. Yes, a therapist. Mary Anne had seen her not long before, after she had become totally depressed. After a few consultations, Mary Anne was on the right track again and felt much better.

I looked at the clock. It was time to wrap up.

"George, I don't think you're going to find what you need on a call-in show," I said gently. "You need to talk to someone professional."

"You mean, like a — "

"A therapist. Don't worry. It doesn't mean you're crazy or anything, George. It will really help. Stay on the line, okay? When we go off the air, I'll give you the phone number of someone very good."

"Okay."

I gave a little closing speech. The red light went off, and Bob came running in with a Stoneybrook phone book. I flipped through and found Dr. Reese's number.

"George, are you still there?"

"Yeah."

"Call Dr. Reese at 555-7660, okay? Just talk to her for awhile. Tell her how you're feeling."

"Okay." I could hear the sniffling again. "Thanks, Claudia."

"Good luck, George."

Click.

When he hung up, I slumped back in my chair. Ashley was giving me a worried look. Bob was sipping coffee. The engineers were busily adjusting dials.

Next to Bob, Mr. Bullock was leaning against a file cabinet. "Congratulations, you two," he said. "You covered for an emergency. You figured out a suitable replacement. You performed a valuable service."

"Thanks," I said.

"Don't thank me," Mr. Bullock said with a chuckle. "Up until now, you've been doing a good show. Tonight, you became professionals."

I turned to Ashley. The color was returning to her face.

This time, when she looked at me, I saw nothing but admiration.

Which, at that moment, was just what I needed.

Friday

Tonight I sat for Marilyn and Carolyn Arnold. They were upset about the "twins" segment on Claud's show. They thought they should have been the ones to do it.

Boy, were they heartbroken. Devastated. I told them they shouldn't be. They hadn't even tried out! But that didn't work. I had to think of something. I had to give them hope.

So I did....

Heartbroken? Devastated?

I think Kristy was going a little overboard. According to her, Carolyn and Marilyn were moping around the house that Friday afternoon. (Later, when I talked to Marilyn, she said they were reading *Jeremy Thatcher, Dragon Hatcher* to each other in the den and laughing out loud.)

Then Kristy found out how "upset" they were and calmed them down. (Carolyn's version was different. *She* said Kristy started talking about my show out of the blue and hinted that the Arnold twins would have made better guests than the other twins.)

Marilyn and Carolyn are eight years old. They are identical in appearance, but definitely not in personality. They used to disagree about everything. Once they actually divided their bedroom in half with masking tape. Fortunately, their parents moved them into separate rooms, and now they tolerate each other much better.

Most of the time.

Anyway, I'll pick up the story of Friday a little further on — at the point where Kristy's version started matching the twins'.

"Claudia was so cool in that call-in," Marilyn said. "That was the best show."

"Oh, boring. I liked the one about families," Carolyn volunteered.

"If I did the shows," Kristy said, "I'd have more humor in them."

"You should try out for that show, Kristy," Carolyn said. "You'd be great."

"I did try out," Kristy replied. "Twice. But Claudia rejected me."

Marilyn's eyes widened. "And she's your *friend*!"

"Hey, I'm not insulted," Kristy insisted. "I have more ideas. Great ones, too. If I can find a couple of helpers."

(She is so sly, isn't she?)

"How about us?' Marilyn asked.

"Yeah!" Carolyn piped up.

Bingo. Kristy was in business again. "All right. I was thinking of, 'Marilyn and Carolyn and Kristy and the Major League Mystery.' Like, we go to a ballgame and a player is missing and we have to find him."

The twins just stared at her. "That's pretty stupid," Marilyn said.

"Or maybe, 'Stoneybrook — a Tour,' " Kristy barreled on. "We could talk about our favorite places, mention the library and some of the restaurants."

"Boring, boring, I am snoring," was Carolyn's critique.

"Kristy, we have to think of something *kids* will like," Marilyn said.

"Like what?" Kristy asked.

"Dolls," Marilyn suggested.

Kristy shook her head. "That probably leaves out most of the boys."

"Good," Carolyn shot back.

"What about sports?" Kristy asked.

Carolyn made a face. "Gross. Let's do something about movies."

"Someone's already doing that," Kristy said.

Carolyn thought for a moment. "I know! A game show, like *Jeopardy*."

Marilyn rolled her eyes. "Too hard."

Kristy saw a copy of *Jeremy Thatcher* lying open on the couch. "What about book reviews?"

The girls looked at Kristy as if she had suggested a foot-smelling contest.

"A book *reading*?" Kristy quickly suggested.

"Yeah!" cried Marilyn.

"I still think we should do a game show," Carolyn said, pouting.

"Why not do both?" said the Great Stoneybrook Idea Machine.

Twin blank stares.

"I could read aloud for awhile," Kristy went on. "You know, something short and fun, like *Where the Wild Things Are*. Then we could put on a *Jeopardy*-type show — about kids' books! We provide the answers, and the listeners call in to guess the questions."

"Yes!" Carolyn shouted.

"But Jeopardy has categories," Marilyn reminded them. "This is all one category."

"Not necessarily," Kristy replied. "We could have 'Books That Have Been Made into Movies,' 'Romance Books,' 'Mysteries' . . ."

" 'Picture Books' and 'Chapter Books,' " Carolyn offered.

"And then, at the end," Marilyn said, "we give the winner a grand prize, maybe a vacation to Bermuda!"

"Uh, it has to be something we can afford," Kristy explained.

"A trip to Washington Mall?" Carolyn said.

"I was thinking of a gift certificate for an ice-cream sundae," Kristy suggested, "or a movie ticket."

"Oh, all right," Carolyn agreed.

"I want to ask the questions!" Marilyn called out.

"You mean, give the answers," Carolyn corrected her. "See, *I'm* the one who knows how to play, so *I* should — "

"You can take turns," said Kristy the Peacemaker, rising from the den sofa. "Okay, we don't have much time. Let's get to work."

The three of them went into the kitchen.

The twins found a pad and pencils in a drawer.

Over the next hour, Kristy and the girls picked five categories and thought up questions (I mean, *answers*) for each.

I saw them that Monday.

Ashley and I were blown away. We were preparing our fifth show, and our topic was "What Are You Reading?"

Guess what?

We said yes. Kristy's dream had come true.

Maybe now she'd leave me alone.

CHAPTER 13

"Ready, Claudia? Ashley? Guests?" Mr. Bullock asked from inside the glass booth.

"Ready," we replied.

"Ready, Mr. Garber?"

Theodore "Ted" Garber, author of the spooky, creepy, gross, and super-popular series *Night Frights*, cleared his throat and said, "Ready!"

I was still in shock. The week before, Ashley had been dying to get a real, live author on the show. She'd heard that Mr. Garber lived in Connecticut. On Friday she tried to invite him to the show, by calling his publishing company.

She did not expect that he'd call back on Saturday and say yes.

(I have to admit, I don't read *Night Frights*, but it felt very cool to be in the same room with a famous author.)

The engineer held up his arm. The red light

went on. "Hellllo, it's a warm, gorgeous, fantastic Thursday, and welcome to 'For Kids Only'! This is Claudia Kishi, sitting with Ashley Wyeth, as always, and we have the coolest, most innnn*cred*ible show for you today!"

Not bad, huh? I was getting better and better at this stuff.

"Today's theme," Ashley continued, "is 'What Are You Reading?' Later we'll have a call-in quiz show — a Junior *Jeopardy* based on kids' books. We'll also have Regina, Cathy, and David, three seventh-graders who are collecting their own strange and spooky stories."

"And in the middle," I said, "for a full half hour, we'll have our surprise guest, who will read from his new book, *Night Frights Number Thirteen: Don't Get Out of Bed!* Yes, fans, we have for you, here in the studio, live and in the flesh . . . Mr. Ted Garber!"

"BOOO-AHHH-HAHHH-HAAAAHHH!"

I nearly jumped through the ceiling. Ashley let out a gasp.

Through the glass I saw the engineers snickering and looking guilty. I guess that was their idea of fun — scaring innocent people with unexpected spooky sound effects.

So weird. I just glared at them.

"Uh, and now, take it away, Regina, Cathy, and David!" Ashley said.

Mr. Garber was smiling sympathetically at

116

me. He looked as if he'd been scared, too (which I found very funny).

Well, the storytelling trio got off to a rocky start. (I think Mr. Garber made them a little nervous.) But their final story was fantastic. It was called "Kokolimalayas, the Bone Man," a Native American tale about a boy who defeats a monster made of bones. Kokolimalayas sticks out its chest and defies the boy to shoot. But the boy knows the monster's secret: its heart is in its fingertip. So he points his arrow and *zzzing!* 'Bye-'bye Bone Man.

"Bravo!" Mr. Garber called out when they were done.

They were thrilled by his response. They crowded around to shake his hand as I said, "And now, the guest you've all been waiting for: Misterrrr Ted Garrrrrberrr!"

(That was reverb. The engineers were in a wacky mood.)

"I wish I could talk like that," was the first thing Mr. Garber said. "Maybe then my kids would listen to me."

He performed a funny routine, and then started reading from his book. Off in the waiting room, I could see Kristy and the twins shuffling papers and fidgeting.

After the reading, we "opened the phones," and Mr. Garber answered callers.

At precisely 5:45, Mr. Garber finished up. I

thanked him, gave Kristy a thumbs-up, and announced, "And now it's time for Junior *Jeopardy* with Kristy Thomas, and the tremendous twins, Carolyn and Marilyn Arnold!"

Kristy confidently grabbed the mike and held it right up to her lips. "THOCKHOO CLOFFFO!"

The engineers' eyes bugged out. As they fiddled with dials, I gently pulled the mike farther away from Kristy's mouth.

"Welcome to Junior *Jeopardy*, the game of skill, smarts, and speed!" Kristy said with a huge grin. "Get your pencils out while I read today's topics: Books Made into Movies, Mysteries, Picture Books, Authors, and Timeless Classics. Each caller will pick a topic and we'll give you an answer to a question. If you guess the question, you get a second and third chance. Any caller who gives us three correct questions wins a cool prize! Let's take the first call."

She punched the speakerphone button. "Heyyyy, you're on the air with Kristy! Tell us your name and pick your category!"

(I know. What a ham.)

"Um, Sarah," a small voice replied. "I'll take Picture Books, please."

Marilyn looked down a sheet of legal paper and leaned into the mike. "The famous elephant who is married to Queen Celeste," she said.

"*Babar!*" Sarah squealed.

"Answers must be in the form of a question," Kristy said solemnly.

"Who is Babar?" suggested Sarah.

"*Rrrrrrrright!*" Kristy barked. "You go again!"

"Um — um — what were the other categories?"

Kristy patiently repeated them.

"Okay," Sarah said. "Timeless Classics."

Carolyn's turn. "In this book, three children step through a wardrobe into a wintry land ruled by a witch."

"What is . . . *The Wizard of Oz?*"

"Nooooo! We're sorry. The question is, What is *The Lion, the Witch, and the Wardrobe?*"

"But I haven't read that!" Sarah said.

"You should," was Kristy's reply. "It's great."

She flicked on the next caller. "What's *your* name?"

"Poindexter," a nasal voice said.

"And your category?"

"I pick . . . Kristy Thomas's nose!"

Kristy scowled. "Alan Gray, is that you?"

We heard a burst of wild laughter, then a click.

Typical.

The next caller picked Books Made into Movies. Marilyn gave the answer: "She is the famous nanny who takes care of the Banks children."

"Who is Mrs. Doubtfire!" the caller cried out.

"Nope," Kristy said. "Let's give another caller a chance." She pressed line 3. "Name, please."

"Mary Poppins!" the caller said. "I mean, Sandy Grayson. That's me. And . . . uh, who is Mary Poppins?"

"Yyyyes! Pick another topic!"

"Mysteries."

Carolyn said, "Her best friend's name is Bess and she lives in the town of River — "

"Who is Nancy Drew?" Sandy blurted out.

(I barely held myself back from answering that one.)

"Yyyyes!" Kristy shouted.

"Authors," Sandy picked.

"He wrote *Jeremy Thatcher, Dragon Hatcher* and *Jennifer Murdley's Toad*," Marilyn said.

Silence.

Marilyn repeated the answer.

"Who is . . . Dr. Seuss?"

"Nnnnoo! Next caller!"

"Who is Bruce Coville?"

"Yyyyyyou got it!" Kristy replied. "What's

your name and your next category?"

Kristy was flying. Carolyn and Marilyn looked as if they were having the time of their lives.

The fifteen minutes went by fast. The only embarrassing moment was when a caller didn't recognize one of Mr. Garber's books.

Mr. Garber grabbed a tissue and pretended to cry. We tried not to crack up. He's pretty cool.

Eventually three contestants did win prizes. When we finally ended the show, Kristy hopped around the room, whooping and pumping her fists.

"Eeeee! Eeeee! Eeeee!" Carolyn and Marilyn sounded like screaming parakeets as they hugged each other and jumped up and down.

The show which came on after ours was using a different studio, so Ash and I could hang out with Bob for awhile after our guests left. We had already planned our sixth and seventh shows (themes: "Music" and "Hobbies"), but not our eighth.

I think we had been avoiding it. Number eight was our last.

The problem was, we hadn't used some of the talented kids who'd auditioned, because they hadn't fit into any of our themes.

"I can think of themes for all of them," Ash

said with a sigh. "But we'd need a few more shows. I wish we could just keep going."

"Me, too," I replied. "Maybe we could call the last show 'Weird Talents' or something. Just let it be a grab bag of acts."

"You want my opinion?" Bob asked.

"Sure," I said.

"Your call-in segment — the one you did on the spur of the moment? Kids have been calling us, asking if you'll do it again."

"Great!" Ashley said. "We can do half weird acts, and half 'Ask Dr. Claudia.' "

"No way," I said.

Ashley gave me a puzzled look. "Why not?"

"You mean, 'Ask Dr. Claudia and Dr. Ashley,' " I reminded her.

Her face lit up. "Deal."

CHAPTER 14

" 'Bye, Dad," I called as the car drove away from the station.

"Good luck!" he replied.

Ash and I waved and watched him leave. Then we stood in the parking lot for a moment. Neither of us moved. We just stared silently at the squat, tan building.

Today was the Saturday of our last show. I didn't feel like rushing things, and I could tell Ashley didn't, either.

Everything had happened so fast. It was hard to imagine only a month had passed since I'd first met Mr. Bullock. All my memories were so fresh. Frantically writing my essay. Sitting in Mr. Bullock's office for the first time, petrified. Seeing Ashley walk in. Feeling absolutely horrified.

"Well, I guess this is it," Ashley said softly. "Shall we?"

"Wait," I said. "I have a secret to tell you."

She turned toward me. Her eyes were moist. I could tell she was feeling just as nostalgic as I was.

"I didn't think this would work. The show, I mean. You and me trying to get along."

Ashley smiled. "Neither did I. No one told me you'd been the first-place winner. When Mr. Bullock brought me into the office, I almost walked back out."

"I almost quit."

We both nodded and looked at the ground. "Well," I said finally, "I feel really stupid about that now. I was wrong."

"Yeah. Me, too."

We shared a smile. Then we put our arms around each other's shoulders and walked into the station.

The door was unlocked, but the reception room was empty and the light was out.

"Are we early?" I asked.

"I don't think so," Ashley replied.

"Hey, there they are!" Mr. Bullock's voice boomed into the room. He was standing in the hallway with a handful of cassettes and CDs.

"Sorry about the lights," he said. "Max isn't here today. He's only working weekdays now. Come on in."

As we walked past Mr. Bullock's office, I noticed three cardboard boxes stuffed with old vinyl records and cassettes. Mr. Bullock dropped his handful in a box. "We're clearing out some old stuff. Selling it to a collector." He exhaled. "Gosh, I hate to see some of this stuff go."

Ash and I gave each other a Look. We knew why he was doing all this — cutting back Max's hours, selling old stuff. He needed to raise money for WSTO.

Either that or he'd just given up. Maybe he was going to sell the rest of the station's collection, too.

I hoped not. Bob had been running a tape of his editorial all week. His article had appeared in the Wednesday edition of the *Stoneybrook News.* It was very well-written. Maybe help would soon be on the way.

"Bob, do you think we really need that third reel-to-reel machine?" Mr. Bullock called into the conference room.

Then again, maybe not.

Bob bustled into the hallway. "Hey, guys, ready for your swan song?"

Huh? I didn't remember any animal acts.

"Your last show," he explained. "That's what swan song means. The song of the dying swan is supposed to be beautiful. How do you feel?"

"Like a dying swan," I said.

"We're totally depressed," Ashley added.

Bob smiled. "Uh-oh. They've been bitten by the bug. Watch out, radio world."

Together we entered the studio. The engineers, as usual, grunted hello and just kept on working. I wondered if they'd even realized how important this show was to us.

Then I found out.

"Claud," Ashley said, "where'd this come from?"

I looked around her and saw a gorgeous bouquet of flowers on our table. "Wow."

Ash found a card tucked inside. She held it out and read it aloud. "To the most wonderful radio hosts we have ever worked with, the WSTO engineers."

"Should auld acquaintance be forgot . . ."

Suddenly the schmaltzy old New Year's song was blaring over the studio speakers. The engineers had risen to their feet and were singing along, holding up glasses full of a clear, bubbly liquid. With a big smile, Mr. Bullock walked toward us with two glasses and a bottle of ginger ale.

I turned to Ashley. She turned to me. It was waterworks time. Tears galore.

Mr. Bullock gave us a hug. We drank our ginger ale.

At the end of the song, Mr. Bullock announced, "Okay, crew, we have a job to do!"

It was hard to get back on track. But soon

the guests began arriving, and we had to greet them, prepare a sequence, and do all the other million things we'd learned to do before a show.

Our first guest was (finally) Sarah Sutton, the backward talker. After that, we had four kids called the Curious Quartet, who played the banjo, the tin whistle, the Jew's harp, and the washboard. Then Rob Miller, an eighth-grader from Stoneybrook Day School, told the strangest story: every time he reached a syllable that sounded like a number, he added *one* to it. (*Won*der became *two*der, *tou*can became *three*can, and so on.) He began the story, "Twice upon a time, there was a twoderful garden full of blossoming threelips." Ashley's favorite part was when a character said, "Elevennis, anytwo?"

I liked the no-structure approach to this show. It was fun. I didn't have to keep thinking of a way to tie everything together.

At five-thirty I announced, "And now, welcome to Ask Dr. Claudia . . ."

"And Dr. Ashley," Ashley added.

I could see that all the lines were already lit up. I pressed line 1. "You're on the air."

"Uh, hi, Claudia?" a boy's voice said.

"Yes?"

"Um, do you have . . ."

I could hear giggling in the background. Visions of Alan Gray danced through my head.

"Go on," I said.

"Do you have . . ."

More giggling. I reached for the button.

"A boyfriend?"

My hand froze.

So did my voicebox. I could feel my face turning red. The engineers were cracking up.

Fortunately, the boy hung up before I had a chance to answer.

I quickly pushed line 2. "Hello?" My voice was a high-pitched squeak.

"Hi! My friends and I are taking a vote, and it's tied. Which is better, *The Lion King* or *Aladdin*?"

"*Aladdin*," I replied.

"*The Lion King*," Ashley said.

"Argggggggh!"

I resisted laughing.

"My name is Denise," said the next caller. "I have this little brother? And he is, like, so gross sometimes. Like yesterday, when I had three friends over? He just comes into my room and sits down and starts burping. And he doesn't leave!"

"Have you tried talking to him about it?" Ashley asked.

"Yeah. He answers in, like, burp talk. It is so disgusting."

"You could all stare at him," Ashley suggested, "in total silence."

"He'll just keep doing it."

"Fine. Let him. And just keep staring. Silently. He'll leave, and I bet he won't come back for another try."

Brilliant. Ashley was brilliant. I would have told the girl to throw him out the window.

The next caller sounded as if he were about six years old. "Um, your show is *really* cool."

"Thanks," we answered.

Then, in a teeny, meek voice, he said, "Can both of you come to my house and baby-sit me some time?"

Boy, was I glad Kristy wasn't there. She'd have started grilling him for his address and his parents' names.

Me? I was moved. I said yes and gave him the BSC phone number.

A few calls later, a woman's voice said, "Hello, Claudia and Ashley. My name is Rhonda Hewitt."

"Hello," Ash and I said. The name sounded familiar, but I wasn't sure why.

"I know only children are supposed to call," the woman continued, "but as the mother of one of your callers, I thought this would be okay. My son, George, spoke to you a couple of weeks ago. You remember, the boy who was so upset about his parents separating?"

Hewitt! Of course. I started to feel faint. This could be big trouble. If I remembered correctly, George had said some not-so-nice things about his mom.

"I — " I had to swallow. "I remember."

I looked at the clock. Five fifty-eight. Yikes! What a way to end the last show.

"Well," Mrs. Hewitt continued, "this, as you know, has been a very difficult time for him and my daughter. But I wanted to tell you that your suggestion was wonderful. You made a huge difference in his life. I wanted to thank you personally, and on the air."

Huh?

The cloud around my head was lifting. My stomach stopped slam-dancing inside my rib-cage. "Oh," I said. "Thanks! I mean, you're welcome."

"I've also been hearing and reading about the station's financial trouble, and I think that's a horrible shame. So I'd like to make a donation. I found your fax number and sent you a note on it. The check will follow in the mail."

"Thank you so much, Mrs. Hewitt," I said. "And I wish you the best of luck."

"My pleasure, dear. I wish there were more people like you. 'Bye, now."

" 'Bye."

Twenty seconds left. I felt as if I were floating. "Well, that's it for now. I want to thank Mr. Bullock, Bob, and our crazy engineers for all their help — "

"And all you great listeners!" Ashley said.

"Especially you," I agreed. "I hope you've enjoyed 'For Kids Only.' It's been a lot of fun for me."

"Me, too," Ashley said. "And don't forget, keep listening to WSTO!"

"Good night!"

"Good night!"

I felt a tug when that red light went off. Ashley and I stood up and gave each other a high-five. The engineers broke into applause.

Then the studio door opened, and Mr. Bullock rushed in, carrying a sheet of paper. On his face was a strange expression. "Everybody come look at this," he called out.

Ashley, Bob, one of the engineers, and I peered over his shoulder. It was the fax of Mrs. Hewitt's note.

When I saw the amount of money she pledged, my jaw nearly hit the floor.

"Who-o-oa," Bob said under his breath. "I guess she must be pretty wealthy."

"That'll help the station, won't it?" Ashley asked.

Mr. Bullock nodded. "If this pledge is for

real," he said, "it'll keep us afloat for six months."

"YEEEEEAAAAA!" I screamed. (I couldn't help it.)

"Yyyyyes!" Ashley shouted.

"Hallelujah!" the engineer bellowed.

Bob? He sank quietly into a chair. From the look on his face, you'd think someone had told him he could eat ice cream three times a day for the rest of his life.

"Claudia, phone for you," Mr. Bullock called out. "On my office line."

I had been high-fiving staff members, helping Ashley clear our stuff out of the studio, and chatting happily about Mrs. Hewitt's pledge. I excused myself and walked down the hall to the station manager's office.

"Who is it?" I asked.

Mr. Bullock just shrugged and left the room.

I picked up the receiver and said, "Hello?"

"Hi, Claudia? It's me."

She didn't have to say her name. I hadn't heard the voice in a long time (*too* long) but I'd recognize it anywhere.

"Stacey?" I said. All these feelings — anger, surprise, happiness — were staging a big wrestling match inside of me. I didn't know what to say.

"Your show was great," Stacey remarked.

"You listened to it?"

"I've been listening to every single one, Claud. I thought they were all good. Especially the one about friendship."

"Oh? I . . . mentioned you on that one."

"Yeah. I heard."

Gulp. I had said something wrong. That was why she hadn't called me until now. She'd been insulted. "I — I'm sorry, Stace."

"Sorry about what?"

"Well, I mean, if you thought that was, you know, too private or something."

"No, no, I loved it, Claudia. Really. I was so moved, I cried."

"Really?"

"Well, *yeah*. I mean, all those things you said about friendship — they were so true. You really made me think, Claud. About all my friends and what they mean to me, who the most important people are in my life, stuff like that."

"Stacey, are you trying to tell me something? You didn't break up with Robert, did you?"

Stacey laughed. "No! I just, well, I just hope we can be friends again someday. You and me. That's all."

"Yeah," I said quietly. "Me, too."

Ashley appeared in the doorway with a stack of papers. She smiled and whispered, "When you have a chance, we need to go through these. I'll be in the studio."

"Uh, Stace, I better go," I said into the phone. "See you."

"Okay. 'Bye. And congratulations."

"Thanks."

I walked out of the office and into the studio. The flowers were giving off the most wonderful smell. Ashley was sitting at the table, shuffling through papers with Bob. Next to her on the desk was an enormous Nestle's Crunch bar with the words *For Claudia — With Love and Thanks, Ashley* written on a Post-It note stuck to it.

Ashley looked over her shoulder. "For energy. We still have some work to do."

I laughed. "Thanks, Ash."

I picked up the Crunch bar and sat at the table. I started to rip it open, but instead I just set it back down.

I didn't need it then.

I was feeling fine without it.

About the Author

ANN M. MARTIN did *a lot* of baby-sitting when she was growing up in Princeton, New Jersey. She is a former editor of books for children, and was graduated from Smith College.

Ms. Martin lives in New York City with her cats, Mouse and Rosie. She likes ice cream and *I Love Lucy*; and she hates to cook.

Ann Martin's Apple Paperbacks include *Yours Turly, Shirley*; *Ten Kids, No Pets*; *With You and Without You*; *Bummer Summer*; and all the other books in the Baby-sitters Club series.

Look for #86

MARY ANNE AND CAMP BSC

We had a lull in the phones. Mal finished writing in the notebook. Claudia took a jujube and put it between two potato chips and gulped it down.

I met Mal's eye. "Okay," I said. "We've got a potential problem ahead."

Kristy lifted her head like a bull who's seen a red flag. "What're you talking about? Is one of the kids we baby-sit having trouble?"

"Nope," I said. "The problem is summer."

"Summer is *never* a problem," said Claudia.

Dawn grinned. "I agree. The beaches are warm, school is out, what could be better?"

"Business is going to be better," said Mal. "Think about it!" She explained about camp and the community center and the three week lag between that and the end of school. "Unless we take on more baby-sitters," she concluded, "we may have more work than we can handle."

"Wow, you're right Mal." Kristy looked thoughtful.

"Who else can we get to work with us?" Shannon asked.

The silence built up. Claudia muttered something, then shook her head.

"I could ask some friends at my school if they could help out, but . . ." Shannon's voice trailed off.

Then Kristy's face lit up. "Camp," she said.

We waited.

"Camp," said Kristy again. "Camp BSC. A baby-sitters camp! A day camp! Like the mini-camp you and Dawn once had, Mary Anne."

It was perfect. We knew immediately that it would take care of the problem. If all eight of the current members of the BSC, including Logan and Shannon were counselors, the camp could probably handle about twenty kids. And all our clients would be very happy.

"Perfect," I said aloud.

"Super perfect," echoed Claudia.

The phone ran again. And again. We were kept very busy the rest of the meeting setting up baby-sitting jobs.

It looked like the summer rush had already begun. We'd thought of the idea of Camp BSC just in the nick of time.

Read all the books
about **Claudia**
in the Baby-sitters Club series
by Ann M. Martin

by Ann M. Martin

More titles... ▶

The Baby-sitters Club titles continued...

❑ MG45659-8	#58 Stacey's Choice	$3.50
❑ MG45660-1	#59 Mallory Hates Boys (and Gym)	$3.50
❑ MG45662-8	#60 Mary Anne's Makeover	$3.50
❑ MG45663-6	#61 Jessi's and the Awful Secret	$3.50
❑ MG45664-4	#62 Kristy and the Worst Kid Ever	$3.50
❑ MG45665-2	#63 Claudia's ~~Freind~~ Friend	$3.50
❑ MG45666-0	#64 Dawn's Family Feud	$3.50
❑ MG45667-9	#65 Stacey's Big Crush	$3.50
❑ MG47004-3	#66 Maid Mary Anne	$3.50
❑ MG47005-1	#67 Dawn's Big Move	$3.50
❑ MG47006-X	#68 Jessi and the Bad Baby-Sitter	$3.50
❑ MG47007-8	#69 Get Well Soon, Mallory!	$3.50
❑ MG47008-6	#70 Stacey and the Cheerleaders	$3.50
❑ MG47009-4	#71 Claudia and the Perfect Boy	$3.50
❑ MG47010-8	#72 Dawn and the We Love Kids Club	$3.50
❑ MG45575-3	Logan's Story Special Edition Readers' Request	$3.25
❑ MG47118-X	Logan Bruno, Boy Baby-sitter Special Edition Readers' Request	$3.50
❑ MG44240-6	Baby-sitters on Board! Super Special #1	$3.95
❑ MG44239-2	Baby-sitters' Summer Vacation Super Special #2	$3.95
❑ MG43973-1	Baby-sitters' Winter Vacation Super Special #3	$3.95
❑ MG42493-9	Baby-sitters' Island Adventure Super Special #4	$3.95
❑ MG43575-2	California Girls! Super Special #5	$3.95
❑ MG43576-0	New York, New York! Super Special #6	$3.95
❑ MG44963-X	Snowbound Super Special #7	$3.95
❑ MG44962-X	Baby-sitters at Shadow Lake Super Special #8	$3.95
❑ MG45661-X	Starring the Baby-sitters Club Super Special #9	$3.95
❑ MG45674-1	Sea City, Here We Come! Super Special #10	$3.95

Available wherever you buy books...or use this order form.

Scholastic Inc., P.O. Box 7502, 2931 E. McCarty Street, Jefferson City, MO 65102

Please send me the books I have checked above. I am enclosing $_____ (please add $2.00 to cover shipping and handling). Send check or money order - no cash or C.O.D.s please.

Name _____ Birthdate_____

Address _____

City_____ State/Zip _____

Please allow four to six weeks for delivery. Offer good in the U.S. only. Sorry, mail orders are not available to residents of Canada. Prices subject to change.

Create Your Own
Mystery Stories!

THE BABY-SITTERS CLUB®

MYSTERY GAME!

WHO: Boyfriend   **WHY:** Romance

WHAT: Phone Call   **WHERE:** Dance

Use the special Mystery Case card to pick WHO did it, WHAT was involved, WHY it happened and WHERE it happened. Then dial secret words on your Mystery Wheels to add to the story! Travel around the special Stoneybrook map gameboard to uncover your friends' secret word clues! Finish four baby-sitting jobs and find out all the words to win. Then have everyone join in to tell the story!

THE BABY-SITTERS CLUB®

Claudia · Kristy · Mallory · Stacey · Dawn · Mary Anne · Jessi

Wow! It's really them—
the new Baby-sitters Club dolls!

Your favorite Baby-sitters Club characters have come to life in these
beautiful collector dolls. Each doll wears her own unique clothes and jewelry.
They look just like the girls you have imagined! The dolls also come with their own
individual stories in special edition booklets that you'll find nowhere else.

Look for the new Baby-sitters Club collection...
coming soon to a store near you!

Kenner®